Mandy's Carriage House Saga

Janet Baughman

Tammy
Love Joy, Peace
Janet Baughman

Copyright 2003

All rights reserved. No part of this book may be reproduced in any form, except for brief quotations by a reviewer, without permission from the author or publisher. No part of this book may be reproduced, stored in a retrieval system or copied by mechanical photocopying, recording or other means without permission from the author or publisher.

First Edition

Other books by Janet Baughman:
310 Quail Run
Anderson, SC 29621

Soaring with the Spirit
A Home for Mandy

Cover design by B.J. Baughman

Oh that men would praise the Lord for his goodness, and for his wonderful works to the children of men!

Psalm 107:8

Dedication

To my sister, Linda, whose faith, indomitable spirit and merry heart has enabled her to see the potential for good in troubled teens. Through her Orchard project she is producing the fruits of responsibility and compassion in young lives.

Acknowledgements

Portions of the material describing The Reverend John Adger's life were taken from his autobiography, My Life and Times. Some of the historical events about the South during the Civil War were researched from Walter Edgar's book, *South Carolina, A History* and used by permission of the publisher. The description of the Glebe Street house came from the ninth edition of the booklet *60 Famous Houses of Charleston, South Carolina,* page 55, published in 1984 by The News and Courier and The Evening Post and used by permission. Information about Manson Jolly came from local lore and legend. Bible references are from the King James Version. Cover design by B.J. Baughman.

First and foremost this book is a work of fiction, therefore whereas some names may be recognizable, character development has been drawn from my imagination.

Chapter One

Charleston, June 1863

Mandy straightened her aching back, mopping her sweaty face with a corner of her apron. Although she had wrapped her long, brown hair in braids around her head, and had clothed her boyishly slim body in the coolest work dress she owned, the June heat still bothered her.

Working in the garden was normally enjoyable but today the heat and high humidity quickly sapped her energy. To make matters worse, her tomatoes and beans had been picked by an intruder sometime during the night. These days nothing was safe. Many of her friends' fine carriage horses had been 'donated' to the army along with food, clothing and anything else not hidden from view. She had learned to leave her gardens in a disheveled state as they drew less attention that way. Her bushiest shrubs had been transplanted along the fence to hide both Cousin Caroline's exotic plants and the vegetable garden that fed her youngsters.

Food was scarce. Sugar, tea and other imports were especially lacking because Northern war ships had blocked the Charleston harbor causing local supply ships to seek other ports. Word had come to her that one of the vessels blockading the harbor was the side-wheel steamer, the S.S. James Adger, named after the father of the Reverend John Adger of Woodburn plantation who had taken her in when she arrived in Pendleton. James Adger, an Irish immigrant, made his fortune in shipping by investing in the first steam railroad in South Carolina and the first steamship line carrying mail from Charleston to New York. Unfortunately, the S.S. James Adger had been docked in the New York City harbor when the Civil War began. The Union Navy claimed her, renamed her the U.S.S. James Adger, outfitted her with eight thirty-two pound cannons and used her quite successfully against the South. Mandy was glad Mr. Adger had died before discovering the humiliating takeover of his favorite ship.

To compensate for the lack of normal staples, she dried as much fruit as possible and used mashed figs as a sweetener for muffins and cookies. Fortunately, most of the children in her care had lived through hard times before so they ate what was available without complaining. Running a small orphanage was demanding enough without having to cope with rationing, too.

The guns had begun again, sounding like rumbling thunder on the horizon. For weeks now, the streets had been filled with gray uniformed soldiers, many of them recovering from war wounds. The unsettling atmosphere of being watched at every turn made it almost impossible to enjoy socializing. She had even resorted to meeting the younger children after school so they would not have to walk home unsupervised. No matter the consequences, war was a great inconvenience, she thought.

Her musings were abruptly interrupted as Katie, looking fresh as a daisy in a willow green and white striped dress accented with a dark green sash, came sauntering into the garden.

"Miss Mandy, may Beth and I walk down to the river?" she asked, tying the ribbon of a large brimmed straw hat under her chin. "We'll be careful, truly we will." Having just turned fifteen, Katie was anxious to try her wings by subtly presenting herself to society. Her bright red hair, hazel eyes, and hourglass figure caused many a young man to look her way.

"What interests you more, the ships or the sailors in their fancy outfits?" teased Mandy as she watched Katie's face flush in embarrassment. "No, the harbor is off limits for now because I just heard cannon fire coming from that direction. Perhaps a blockade runner is trying to get through. If you feel like walking, would you take Mrs. Cline a jar or two of okra pickles and fig conserve? I understand her cousins from John's Island are staying with her for a while. Probably she can use some extra condiments. Just don't dawdle; there are strange soldiers everywhere. I'm sure they are gentlemen but they aren't Charlestonians. Their customs may be different than ours."

"Yes, ma'am. We'll do anything to get away from these four walls for a while, even walk three blocks to Mrs. Cline's house in this beastly heat. Life is so monotonous. It's the same routine day in and day out." Katie pouted prettily.

"True, but I'd rather live with tedium than be caught in the cross fire of Yankee bullets. Do you want Neal to go with you?"

"No, thank you. All he'd do is stop to talk to every soldier he met to get the latest news about the war. We're not interested in war stories."

"Go on, then. Let me know the minute you return." Mandy resumed her weeding, noticing the okra was growing profusely and would soon need thinning.

Katie, along with Beth, a chubby, excitable ten year old who was delighted to be included, strutted out the gate with exaggerated posturing and walked toward town. As Mandy had said, there were Confederate soldiers everywhere. Some exuded dignity while others looked as wild as the wilderness from which they had come. One man had a gray beard hanging almost to his stomach and hair in a braid dangling halfway down his back. Beth was mesmerized by his appearance and, walking backward the better to see him, bumped into another soldier who was loitering at the edge of the street.

"Excuse me, sir, " she said, taking in his sweat-stained uniform and unshaven face. "I wasn't looking where I was going. Sorry."

"Sorry, is it? You might have knocked me in front of that team of four, maiming me for life. I need some compensation for your ill manners, girl, indeedy I do," growled the soldier, eyeing them with distaste. "I'll just help myself to a hank of your friend's hair. That bright red braid will look mighty fine tied to my rifle. Much classier than an Injun scalp." In one fluid motion he unsheathed his knife and reach for Katie's long braid which was hanging beneath her hat.

"Run, Katie, run!" screamed Beth, dropping the basket of goodies she had been carrying, as she snatched up her skirt and dashed down the sandy path.

Frantically Katie twisted away from the soldier's grasp and sprinted up to Beth. "Head for St. Phillip's church. It's just around the corner," she gasped, grabbing Beth's hand and pulling her along. Too afraid to even look back to see if they were being followed, the frightened girls burst through the double wooden doors of the church, ran down the aisle and hid behind the altar.

"Here, here! What's all this noise?" asked Reverend McMurtry, who was just entering the sanctuary. "Why, Katie, Beth. What ails you?"

"A soldier tried to cut off Katie's hair," babbled Beth, hysterically. "We thought he was chasing us. Did you see anyone else come in?"

"Nary a soul. More than likely he was just teasing you. Katie's carrot red hair draws many people's attention. When you've gotten your breath and composure, I'll walk you home." Since his sermon preparation was going badly, he was glad for the excuse to quit. He waited while both girls smoothed their dresses and retied their bonnets.

"I dropped the basket we were suppose to take to Mrs. Cline. I guess we'd better go back the way we came in case it's still there," whispered Beth to Katie.

"I hope he took the stuff as a fair trade for my hair. I don't want that soldier to come after me again," replied Katie, anxiously. "Here, Beth, help me tuck my braid under my hat. As soon as I get home I'm going to cut it off."

"Don't you dare, young lady," admonished the kindly pastor. "The scriptures say a woman's hair is her glory. Yours is exceptionally beautiful. God has smiled on you in a very special way, giving you such vibrant red hair. Now, if you both are ready, let us be on our way. I have a meeting in forty-five minutes." Placing an arm around each girl, he ushered them out the door and set off at a brisk pace. When they reached the site of the encounter with the soldier, they searched carefully but the basket could not be found. Katie breathed a sigh of relief.

"Miss Mandy! Katie was threatened by a horrid, old soldier!" shouted Beth, as they entered the garden where Mandy was still viciously chopping weeds. "He wanted to cut off her braid but we ran as fast as we could to St. Phillips and hid in the vestry. Reverend McMurtry walked us home from there." Beth chattered on excitedly while Katie's ashen face and wide eyes betrayed the fear she was trying to contain.

"Are you all right?" Mandy gathered Katie's trembling body in her arms and gently patted her back while Reverend McMurtry stood to one side, watching.

"Tis a sad day in Charleston when men be so bold as to confront a young girl in plain daylight. No young woman should walk about without the protection of a gentleman during these turbulent times," he said, glancing at Mandy with a look of concern and warning.

"But the girls only went to take Mrs. Cline some fig conserve and okra pickles. She lives less than three blocks away. Oh, when will this accursed war end? If women were running the country we'd find a civilized way to settle disputes instead of this everlasting fighting! Plague take it! Excuse me, Reverend. My patience is running thin." Mandy blushed with embarrassment at her ungodly outburst.

"I understand, my dear. What with eight mouths to feed, and growing bodies to clothe, 'tis only natural you have anxious moments. I wish St. Phillips could help but our refuge house is bursting at the seams with fatherless families whose lands and possessions have been destroyed by the Yankees. I heard today that another major conflict is soon to take place just north of here. I fear many more good lives will be lost. I ask the Almighty daily to end this ghastly slaughter before the flower of Southern manhood is destroyed forever."

"If only the Citadel cadets had not fired on that Union ship, Star of the West,[1] perhaps this war would never have

---

[1] Edgar, South Carolina, A History; University of SC press, 1998 P.357

begun," complained Mandy, who still vividly remembered the January day in 1861 when the first cannon fire was heard.

"Tempers had been smoldering in Southern hearts ever since the heavy taxes were levied on our exports by the Northern states. Sooner or later it was bound to come to a head," replied Rev. McMurtry. "Remember the surrender of Fort Sumter? People came from miles around to watch the skirmish. Some even brought picnic baskets. It seemed more like a carnival than a battle."[2]

"I remember the cheering when the Yankees gave up the fort. Who would have thought a month later Union ships would blockade our harbor. Now Port Royal is under the Northern army's thumb and many of the plantation owners have come to stay with relatives and friends in Charleston.[3] I think we had better rename The Holy City, the Starving City." Mandy shook her head in despair as she thought of all the suffering that had taken place during the past few years. Besides the war, a fire had destroyed five hundred forty acres of buildings in the city including the unique circular Congregational Church, St. John's Cathedral and St. Andrews Hall.[4]

" Miss Greene, I think it best if the children remain behind these walls. I will send a man to escort you twice a week so you may do the necessary shopping and attend vespers. In the meantime, if you need help, send one of the boys to me at St. Phillips. 'Tis the safest solution, don't you agree?" The Reverend's emphasis on the word 'safest' jolted Mandy's thoughts back to the present situation.

Mandy nodded. "I should have thought of that myself. I suppose I rely on Katie too much because she is so trustwor-

---
[2] Edgar, South Carolina, A History; University of SC press, 1998 P.358
[3] Edgar, South Carolina, A History; University of SC press, 1998 P.360
[4] Edgar, South Carolina, A History; University of SC press, 1998 P.361

thy and intelligent. I never worry about her not completing a task. I see her inner beauty but have overlooked the fact that she is growing into a beautiful young woman as well. Thank you for your wise counsel, Reverend. I shall abide by your suggestions."

With a reassuring smile Reverend McMurtry turned quickly and walked away. He wished St. Phillips had not agreed to rent Number Six Glebe Street to Miss Greene. But the funds were provided for in her cousin's will so it was a matter of honoring the request of the now deceased Cornelia Thompson. Besides, at the time who could foresee a war as brutal as this?

At the moment the countryside was over run by the military. It was only a matter of time before the fighting would intensify in the city. What would Mandy do then to protect her fledglings, Rev. McMurtry wondered. It was all in the hands of the Almighty. At the moment prayer was the only recourse. He felt the weight of his calling as he reentered the church.

After supper Mandy called a family meeting. Soon eight pairs of eyes were anxiously fastened on her, watching every move she made in an attempt to interpret her body language. Mandy smiled and slowly smoothed out her dress as she sat, trying not to show fear or undue concern. She gazed fondly at the orphaned children before her.

Neal, fourteen, was tall and thin with a shock of straight dark hair that constantly fell over his brown eyes. At his age he seemed to be all elbows and knees, with a voice that ranged from squeaky tenor to bass. Coming from a dysfunctional family that disintegrated before the start of the war, he struggled in his efforts to be the man of the house.

John, twelve, was blond and pudgy; a follower who

dogged Neal's every step. He had a sweet nature and usually was willing to do whatever he was told.

Sam was the same age as Beth. A born naturalist, he marched to the rhythm of his own drum, spending most of his spare time outside playing with animals or collecting bugs. He had sandy red hair, freckles, and a pixie face that invited others to share their problems with him. He was definitely a devil-may-care, high-energy person.

Alex, at seven, was painfully shy. Mandy was certain he had been either physically or verbally abused as a small child. He was happiest when playing alone or given some small task he could complete on his own. He was a handsome lad with regular features and a wide grin that was all the more noticeable because he rarely smiled.

Lizzie, five, had dark wavy hair, eyes of violet and a round face with apple cheeks. Like Beth, she had a tendency to be a chatterbox, voicing her own undisputable opinions, which often set her at odds with the other children. One never knew what she would say next.

Susan was Mandy's golden girl. She had sunny yellow curls, big blue eyes, a porcelain complexion and a babyish nature. She had been slow to speak and, at age three, still used short sentences. Like John, she was a follower and toddled after Lizzie or Katie constantly. She was happiest when sitting in someone's lap, which she managed to do often because even new acquaintances were attracted to her baby-doll features.

"Rev. McMurtry was here to see if we had any needs after he walked Beth and Katie home from their errand," Mandy began, avoiding any mention of the soldier. No doubt Beth already had painted an exaggerated picture of the morning's event. "He suggested we stay in the private areas of our garden behind the fence because of the unusual numbers of unwanted visitors in the city. I think that is a good idea. I feel very safe here but it's best to avoid prying eyes. Why don't we make the center lower-level room of our house into a playroom? It's so much cooler there. It would mean you boys would have to share bedrooms. Do you mind, Neal, John?"

"No, ma'am," they chorused, poking each other to establish dominance.

"Could we put some of our outdoor toys in there?" asked Alex, who had built a miniature fort under a sprawling live oak and spent most of his time playing soldier.

"I will designate certain play areas for each of you. You may use them as you wish as long as you do not bring any wild creatures inside," Mandy replied with a warning look at Sam, who had an impressive collection of live bugs living in the shrubbery near the back door.

"Let's begin right now. Everybody downstairs. Girls, you remove the bedding and carry the linens to Neal's room. Boys, you dismantle the beds and carry your chests to their new locations. Alex will move in with John, Sam with Neal. I will help you arrange the furniture so each of you will have a special place. What fun! I just love projects!" The more enthusiasm the better, Mandy thought, jumping up from her chair.

The rest of the day was spent rearranging rooms. Soon the large center room of the lower level held toys and games instead of beds. Its central location meant even the noisiest play would be partly muffled from outside ears.

"I must make a secret room in which to hide the girls, if necessary," Mandy said to herself as she surveyed the new playroom. God forbid soldiers would ever enter the house unbidden but this was war and not everyone played by the rules. She remembered the story of a Charleston lady who hid her daughters in the attic while British soldiers occupied her house during the Revolutionary War. Perhaps she should follow suit.

That evening, after the children were in bed, she climbed the steep, narrow spiral staircase tucked between a chimney and the third floor hall and entered the garret room just under the roof. She finally decided the large cedar closet would do. A fake wall with hidden hinges would have to be built on one end where there was a small window to provide light and an opening in the exterior brick wall that would serve as an air vent. She would have Amos construct the wall when he came to help with the heavy chores.

Satisfied she was doing all she could for her brood, she turned her thoughts to other daily demands. She recalled the survival techniques her Indian friend, Soaring Hawk, had taught her and wondered how she could apply them here.

Money was not an issue as the bank sent her the monthly inheritance check of $300 (although it now came in Confederate currency which she detested). The problem was, there was not much left to buy. She and Katie spent much of their time letting out clothing as the boys, especially, seemed to be growing by the minute. She wondered if there was any way to hide a milking goat among the shrubs but decided it's bleating would soon consign it to someone's cook pot.

Fortunately, much of the food she grew could be dried and what remained she preserved or they ate or traded for other necessities. Life was tolerable. Fingering the little silver cross she wore around her neck, a gift from her mother years ago, she mentally recommitted her family to her Lord, trusting Him to continue to meet their basic needs.

"You have not because you ask not," Jesus had said to His disciples. So, when a need arose, she would ask and He would answer.

"'In times of disaster the righteous will not wither; in days of famine they will enjoy plenty'," she quoted from Psalm thirty-seven, adding another verse, "'I have never seen the righteous forsaken or His seed out begging bread.'" Smiling to herself in the confidence that all would be well, she went to bed.

Chapter Two

Mandy tossed restlessly in her sleep as cannon fire from the harbor began in earnest. Suddenly a crash followed by the sound of splintering wood echoed through the night. She jumped out of bed just as Susan and Lizzie dashed into her room.

"Go to the cellar playroom! Hurry!" she ordered, lighting a candle, as one by one the children, frightened by the noise, ran into the hallway. Again a flash appeared in the night sky as another cannon opened fire from the same direction. She guessed supply boats were trying to evade the Union ships blockading the river.

"Are we going to die?" asked Lizzie, burying her head in Mandy's nightgown as another errant cannonball hit a house several blocks away.

"No, we're not going to die. God will protect us. The battle is down at the harbor. We are safe here. Sometimes they just add too much powder to the cannons and the shot travels farther than it should. We should be praying for the soldiers.

They are the ones in danger. I know, let's sing some of the church hymns. That way the cannon fire won't seem so loud. Holy, holy, holy, Lord God Almighty,...." Mandy sang as loudly as she could, swinging one hand to help keep time as she prodded the boys to join in. Hymn after hymn helped drown out the deafening roars of artillery until, her voice hoarse with the effort, Mandy stopped and listened. Except for the muffled voices of people scurrying around outside to evaluate the damage, the night was silent.

"It's over," said Neal, his body slumping with relief. As the oldest boy, he felt he should be the bravest, but the effort often stretched his nerves to the breaking point.

"Everybody back to bed," ordered Mandy quietly. "We've lost a bit of sleep so you can stay in bed a little longer in the morning if you like." She tried to treat the incident as casually as possible to calm emotions.

After an hour of tossing and turning, she fell into a deep slumber. Suddenly a scene from Friendville, the vast plantation area in Pendleton where she had once lived, flitted through her subconscious. She saw herself wandering carefree and barefoot through the fields, while gazing at her beloved mountains covered in blue haze. She woke with a start. Was God telling her to leave Charleston? Should she take the children to Pendleton? Perhaps Smith, her former beau, would allow them to live on his cotton plantation since he had recently built a large carriage house.

"Lord Jesus, please show me if this dream is from You," she prayed. "I need some kind of a sign so I will know I am in Your will. Otherwise, traveling with the children would be too dangerous." Mandy paused, wondering if the train from Charleston to Columbia was still in operation. If so, the first part of the journey would be fairly easy. She would check the train schedule first thing in the morning.

Sleep fled as her mind began planning their escape. She moved to her writing desk and started making a list of supplies they would need for the trip. When the first faint glow of sunrise crept through the shuttered windows she sank to her knees and, resting her head on the needlepoint seat of her chair, prayed for God's will and protection for her children.

As she was cooking breakfast, she heard a tapping at the back door. Who could that be? How did they get into the yard? Nervously she peered through a tiny opening in the shutter. It was Amos, her gardener. Why had he come on the wrong day? Quickly she let him in before other prying eyes could sum up the situation.

"Amos! What are you doing here? I thought you were coming on Thursday."

"Miss Mandy, youse is got to leave the city right away! One of my cousins is fightin' wid de Yankees and came to warn us dey is plannin' an all out attack on Charleston as soon as some general gits here from Virginny, an' he's already on his way. De fightin' will be fierce! No place for younguns. Most folks is headin' fo' Columbia on de train. You needs to go, too, while de train still runnin'. I'se here to hep you pack and tote yer goods to de station." Amos's eyes rolled nervously as he clenched and unclenched his hands repeatedly in his effort to be understood.

"Oh, Amos, God has spoken! Help yourself to the grits and biscuits while I call the children. We will leave as soon as I can gather together some supplies. Let me show you where to hide Cousin Caroline's valuables. There are some loose boards beside the chimney downstairs. Slip everything you can between the walls then nail the boards tight." Mandy ran down to the lower level, shook John awake, pulled his bed from the wall and pointed to several cypress boards. "Wrap the loose silver in blankets so it won't clank if anyone bangs on the wall. I'll get her jewelry, silver tea service and platters."

Bounding back up the stairs she hurried to Katie and Beth's room. "Girls, hurry and finish dressing; wear something plain and dark. Then get the others and have your breakfast. Eat as much as you can then pack the rest. I'll be there in a few minutes."

Mandy hurried up the narrow winding stairs to the attic where she had stored most of her cousin's valuables in a large wooden trunk. Sorting through the clothes and household items she pulled out everything of value that would fit the ten-inch space between the foundation wall and the paneling. The rest Amos would have to bury. Carefully she chose some of the jewelry to take with her in case she needed extra money, then, wrapping everything else of importance in old linens, she rushed down to where Amos was busily filling the hiding space with items from the china cabinet and sideboard.

"Pack these in, too," she said, passing over her bundle. "Perhaps we should put some items in another spot." She searched the walls frantically. "No, I guess not. I don't want someone tearing the whole house down searching for family heirlooms."

While Amos worked diligently, Mandy returned to the kitchen that was now occupied by all the children, busily downing their breakfast. "Amos said we must leave Charleston today because the Yankee soldiers are going to have a major battle near here. Last night was just a preview, I guess. We will take the train to Columbia, then continue on to Pendleton where we will stay with friends.

"Boys, wear some sturdy trousers and take two extra

changes of dark clothes that won't show wear and tear. Roll everything up so they will fit in this valise. Girls, you do the same. Take everyday dark dresses and only one petticoat to wear. Put on your leather shoes and bring a sunbonnet. All your extra clothes must fit in this small trunk. The littlest children may bring one comfort toy each. You older ones select a schoolbook of your liking. Katie and Beth, as soon as you are packed, bake another batch of biscuits, then douse the fire completely. Neal and Sam, gather whatever you can from the garden that is edible. Hurry, now!"

Mandy went to her desk and wrote a short note to Smith LaFarge in Pendleton, telling him of their departure time to Columbia and her plan to buy or rent a wagon to complete the trip to Pendleton. After giving the letter to Amos to mail, she began packing. Remembering her former ordeal helped her prioritize items. Rather than pack large trunks, she decided on one small trunk for clothes then smaller valises which the older children could carry. She remembered how Soaring Hawk had devised a backpack, leaving his hands free. She would follow his method. She added a length of clothesline to her bundle along with soap, two small iron pans, two sharp knives and several metal cups. Jugs filled with drinking water were tied with cord to fit around her waist. Into boxes lined with waxed paper she stuffed as much dried food, preserves, vegetables and bread as would fit. The boys would carry those. As an afterthought she added a small amount of paper money and jewelry to each valise. Better to lose a little than all of it at once, she thought.

By the time she had finished, Katie was filling a basket with fresh ham biscuits and whatever baked goods remained. They would eat well for the first few days, at least. Amos waited patiently until Mandy ushered the children out the door.

They understood the need to leave everything behind and made no protests. Tears filled her eyes as she locked the gate.

"I'll be back. God keep you safe and secure," she whispered to her house. Then blinking the water from her eyes, she smiled brightly and said, "Our wonderful adventure is about to begin. Stay together so you won't get lost. Amos will carry the trunk but each of you is responsible for your own valise."

The streets were already crowded with soldiers and travelers. Fortunately, the train station was just a few blocks away but the closer they got the more crowded the road became. It seemed they weren't the only family leaving Charleston for safer accommodations. Mandy stood in line for tickets while Amos helped the children board the train and stash their bundles. Everywhere trunks by the hundreds were being tied on flat cars and people rushed around shouting for help with their luggage. It seemed all Charleston had gotten news of the advancing Union troops.

Although it was only mid-June, the heat had reached summer proportions. Little rivulets of sweat trickled down Mandy's neck and back soaking her dress. Impatiently she wiped her face, glancing with concern at the long line of people both in front and behind her. Would there be enough room on the train for them all? Each face wore the same expression: desperation and determination. There was no party atmosphere here, the people stood in silence, speechless at having to leave loved ones and family homes.

"One adult and eight children's tickets, please," Mandy said in a pleading voice as she passed a handful of confederate notes toward the ticket master.

"Sorry, ma'am. We're no longer taking paper money. Silver or gold, only. That will be twelve dollars, please." Mandy bit her lip in frustration. She had very few coins and had hoped to use Confederate money along the way. She hastily pulled out a 20 dollar gold piece and pushed it over the counter. The clerk returned eight dollars in paper money along with the tickets.

"But you just said….," began Mandy, indignantly.

"Next!" shouted the ticket master, and before she could protest further she was pushed aside by the anxious family behind her. Deciding this was no time to make a scene, she hurried to the coach where she had seen Amos take the children. Gathering her long skirt in one hand she climbed the steps and began to walk the aisle looking for her brood. The chattering of the passengers relieved to be on board was deafening.

"Miss Mandy! Here we are," shouted John, waving his cap from near the back of the car. Mandy smiled and waved back. Everything was going to be fine.

"Thank you, Amos, for all your help. Would you please check on our house once in a while if you can?" Mandy pressed the eight dollars change she had gotten into the trembling black hand. "Help yourself to whatever grows in the garden, too."

"Yas, um. Youse kin count on ol' Amos. Stay safe an' hurry back," he replied with tears of sorrow in his eyes. Then, clutching the money, he turned and was soon lost in the crowd.

Mandy happily glanced at her wards, mentally counting heads: one, two, three… "Where's Sam?" she asked, bending over the seat back to see if he was playing on the floor.

"He went to the back of the car to watch the soldiers load the flat cars," said Katie. "He promised not to be long."

Mandy hurried to the open doorway and stood on the tiny platform. Sam was nowhere to be seen.

"Sam! Samuel Tate! Please return to your seat," she called again and again over the surging crowd below, but Sam seemed to have vanished. Frantic, she hurried back to the children. "I must find Sam. You children stay in your seats no matter what! Katie, you are in charge. Do not let them out of your sight!" Mandy rushed through the throng of people entering the train, climbed down the steps and ran along side the flat cars, calling for Sam with every breath. The din of men shouting, animals neighing and trunks banging all but drowned out her voice. Fear, her old enemy, began squeezing her throat shut.

"Oh God, help me find Sam! I can't leave without all my children." Dashing past the flatbed carriers, she reached the livestock cars where she heard a familiar voice.

"Miss Mandy! Look at me!" Perched atop one of the Army mules was Sam, a gleeful smile on his face, his hands entangled in mane. "A nice soldier said I could guard his mule until he came back. I can see everything from here."

Mandy breathed a sign of relief. She should have known to look among the animals. He was a lover of anything that had four legs. "Get off the mule, Sam. Be careful. Don't kick him. He'll be fine tied to that post. Hurry, now, we must board the train before it leaves without us." Even as the words left her mouth the train whistle shrilled a warning note for all passengers to prepare for start up. Grasping Sam's hand she ran for the coach, arriving at the door just as the car gave a beginning lurch. Shoving him up the steps onto the platform, Mandy followed as the wheels began their perpetual motion. "Co-lum-bi-a, Co-lum-bi-a," they seemed to sing in an accelerating cadence.

Once settled back on the hard wooden bench seat, Mandy took a deep breath. The air from the open window helped cool her even though tiny granules of soot and ash swirled in the air. How glad she was that the children were dressed in dark clothing so the dirt would not be so noticeable. While the boys hung as far out the window as possible watching in awe the ever-changing scenery, she closed her eyes and centered her thoughts on her beloved Glebe Street house. Truly her house had been a gift from God via her cousin Caroline. She felt so safe and secure within its thick, brick walls. Built in 1770 of Georgian design, it had been originally owned by Bishop Robert Smith, a pastor, who had left his congregation to fight in the Revolutionary War. Upon his return, the first classes of the College of Charleston were held in the very basement rooms Mandy had made into bedrooms and a play area for the boys.

The house had three stories and a garret room under the roof. With four main rooms on each floor, there was plenty of room for the children without sacrificing her needed privacy. How she loved the cypress paneling, the high ceilings and the spacious center hall. The tall, narrow windows on every side furnished plenty of light and when open brought in even the slightest cooling breeze from the bay. An added bonus was the cistern just outside the front entrance that caught the rain from the roof. Wash water was always at her fingertips. Her reverie was broken abruptly by Susan's announcement that she had to go potty. It was time to concentrate on reality.

Five hours later, following a series of stops and a hasty lunch that left biscuit crumbs and jam smears on the children's faces, there was a sudden screeching of brakes and a jerking motion that almost flung them from their seats. Neal leaned out the window as far as he could to see if he could detect the problem.

"I see several men with red flags talking to the engineer,"

he reported. "It looks as if there is a pile of rubble or something along side the train."

Within minutes a conductor appeared beside their car and shouted, "Everybody out. The tracks have been torn up just ahead. This is as far as we can go, folks. Sorry. Blame the Yankees for the disruption."

"How far are we from Columbia?" Neal yelled at the railroader's disappearing back.

"About five miles," he shouted back.

"Don't move," ordered Mandy, as passengers around them pushed and shoved their way to the exits. "Let's just wait until this melee had passed. I'm afraid I'll lose some of you in this crowd. All we have to claim is one trunk. Since it's only five miles into town, we'll be there before dark."

When the crowd thinned, Mandy sent Neal and John to retrieve their trunk while the rest of the children fidgeted in their seats. After what seemed like an eternity, the boys appeared outside the train window.

"We found it!" exclaimed John, proudly. "The yellow ribbon tied on the handle really helped. We knew which was our trunk right away."

"Stay there. We'll come to you," said Mandy, grasping Lizzie and Susan's hands and herding everyone down the steps of the train.

"Do you boys think you can each take a side handle and carry the trunk as far as Columbia? Katie and I will spell you off when you get tired." Mandy stared anxiously at the trunk which now looked five times larger than it had when she was packing it.

"It's not that heavy, we can do it," boasted Neal, grabbing the metal handle on his side. "Come on, John, heave to." Swaggering and staggering, the boys set off in the direction the crowd was going. Mandy, ordering everyone to stay close together, followed, carrying Neal's valise under one arm and John's in the opposite hand.

The five miles to Columbia seemed more like five thousand. Lizzie and Susan soon tired and whined to be carried. Time was spent switching baggage among the older children so she could give Susan piggy-back rides or carry Lizzie for a few hundred yards. The heat was stifling. If anything it seemed hotter and more humid here than in Charleston. Soon everyone was drenched in sweat. It wasn't long before the main body of travelers was far ahead of them. Twice they had to stop so everyone could have a drink of water and rest their aching arms.

Just when Mandy felt she could not take another step, the train station came into sight. She eased her way past people loitering on the platform and went to the ticket window.

"Excuse me," she asked the man behind the bars. "Is there a livery stable in town where I might rent a horse and buggy?"

"Ma'am, the livery closed over a year ago. The soldiers took most of the horses. Even mules are scarcer than hen's teeth. The only way to travel is by long shanks," he replied, pointing to his legs. "Unless you've friends or relatives, of course."

Mandy bit her lower lip in frustration. If the trek to the station was any indication of what lay ahead….. She tried to remember the name of the people the Gibbes had stayed with here years ago, when they were returning to Beaufort, but she had not paid that much attention then, wanting only to remain unnoticed. Well, this situation called for an immediate decision. She and the children could never manage the trunk that held extra clothes; she would have to leave that. She approached the ticket master again. "Would it be possible to leave this trunk here for several weeks? It seems my plans have changed and it is no longer needed."

"We have a baggage room where you can stash it but I'll not guarantee its safety. These are troublesome times. Besides the soldiers, we have many destitute people roaming about who will steal anything not nailed down. Can't blame them much, most have had their livestock and farm produce confiscated by the army. To them turn-about seems fair play."

Mandy nodded. The scenario was all too familiar, but she had no other choice. Calling John and Neal, the three of them carried the trunk into a corner of the baggage room where it would be less noticeable. Then, opening another large valise containing everyday attire, she doled out equal amounts to the four oldest. "Roll up these clothes into small parcels and tuck them in your cases wherever they will fit. Do the best you can. We'll walk until God provides another mode of transportation. When you get tired, say so and we'll stop and rest. Much of the food will be gone by tonight so tomorrow your packs will be lighter." She placed the empty valise beside the trunk.

"Wasn't the train ride fun! The trees went by so fast I couldn't see any birds in them," said Sam. " I bet we could go across the whole country in just a week on a train."

"Life is full of pleasant surprises," replied Mandy, happy to hear Sam and the others say something positive. "Now our greatest adventure begins. On to Pendleton, troops." She purposely kept her voice cheerful. "It's not too far away so we will walk a bit every day and soon we will be with some of my dearest friends."

"But where will we sleep?" asked Beth, anxiously. She was not one for outdoor excursions. Every shadow was a monster, every snake a deadly viper to her timid nature.

"There are several families along the way that I know. I'm sure they will be more than happy to put us up." If I can remember where they live, Mandy thought to herself. It would be a miracle if she could find the families she had stayed with on her trip from Pendleton to Beaufort. With her nose in one of Mr. Gibbes' history books she had paid little attention to landmarks or people.

Now her greatest fear was meeting Union soldiers or deserters who might take advantage of her and the children. Suddenly, the words of the 23rd Psalm rose up from within her with a divine assurance that all would be well.

"Thank You, Lord Jesus," she whispered to the wind. Then, setting her hat at a jaunty angle and squaring her shoulders, she began the walk to her future with eight pairs of feet trudging along behind her.

Chapter Three

Since it was still afternoon, Mandy decided to try to get the children away from the maddening confusion of the city. They walked for about two hours, rested, drank some water and ate dried figs, then plodded on. An hour later, she recognized a white, clapboard house set back among large, long-needled pine trees. She remembered it from her previous journey as a genteel boarding house.

"Let's see if we can stay here tonight," she said, turning into the sandy carriage road. "Um. What was the lady's name? I recall she had fiery red hair and wore only black silk dresses. O, something. O'Conner, O'Leary, no, O,O, O'Laughlin! That's it. Mrs. O'Laughlin from County Clare, Ireland."

By this time they were on the large covered porch. The house seemed unusually quiet for that time of evening. Mandy rapped sharply on the door. No answer. She tried again. Her eye caught a tiny flicker of a curtain in a far window.

"Mrs. O'Laughlin! It's Mandy Greene, a friend of Doctor

and Nana Stewart of Pendleton! We stayed with you several years back on our way to Beaufort. Do you remember? My children and I need lodging for the night. Can you help us?" Mandy's loud voice echoed down the porch. She was sure someone was watching from within. She glanced around for signs of a military presence but could see none.

Finally there was the screech of a metal door hinge. "Go away. I no longer offer lodging," rasped a fearful voice.

"Please, Mrs. O'Laughlin. It's almost dark and I have eight children who are weary from traveling all day. Please help us. I can pay," Mandy pleaded.

After a moment the door opened a little wider.

"Let me see you. ALL of you."

Mandy and the children filed obediently past the narrow door opening.

"I've no food. You will have a bed; nothing more."

"That will be fine. We just need some shelter for the night. We have food which we will be glad to share with you," replied Mandy, relieved to have found lodging.

There was another long lapse, then the door slowly swung open to reveal the occupant of the house. Mandy could not prevent a gasp as she saw Mrs. O'Laughlin's face.

"Dear Mrs. O'Laughlin, what has happened to you?"

"It was the Yankees, blast'em. They stole my horses and when I shot at them, they shot back. Nearly killed me, they did. The bullet entered one side of my face and came out the other, damaging the nerves. That accounts for the scars and droopy mouth. Then they set fire to my stables. I've nothing left but the house. Recently I've learned that my son, my only son, is missing in action. I feel so helpless I wish I were dead." Her voice betrayed the anguish of spirit that her face could no longer disclose.

"Miss Mandy says Jesus loves everyone, especially widows and orphans. We're orphans but Jesus loves us. He loves you, too," said Lizzie boldly, looking to Mandy for reassurance.

"Of course He does, Mrs. O'Laughlin. He has led us to you. You are keeping us from sleeping in the wilderness unprotected. We need your hospitality very much. Children, please follow this kind lady. She will show you where to put your things." Mandy felt action would divert her hostess from another outburst of grief. As if on cue, led by Katie, the children introduced themselves to the distraught woman who then took them upstairs to two large, front bedrooms.

"Boys on the left; girls on the right. Linens are in this highboy," she instructed, pointing to a massive walnut dresser. "Make your own beds. I'll put the kettle on for tea."

Her voice already sounds stronger, thought Mandy as she watched the matron descend the steps and hurry to the kitchen.

"Come along, Miss Greene. I must confess I do not remember you in particular but I do recall the nice visit I had with the Stewarts and the Gibbes. Do tell me the latest news about them. Are they well? Are the rumors true? Have the Yankees taken over the Low Country?"

Mandy gave her the latest news about the war effort in Charleston and the surrounding areas but kept the report as upbeat as possible, making her retreat sound more like a minor inconvenience than a major challenge. She had not heard from the Gibbes since the start of the war so she had little to share about them.

As Mrs. O'Laughlin brewed the tea, Mandy set out the food from the box Sam had been carrying: ham biscuits, dried fruit, bread and a jar of grape preserves. The children noisily pulled chairs to the table then waited quietly for the blessing.

"Dear Jesus, thank You for a safe trip so far. Bless this house and Mrs. O'Laughlin. Please comfort her and provide for her needs now and forever. Bless this food to our bodies' use and us to Thy service. Amen." Out of concern for the children's rumbling stomachs, Mandy kept the prayer short and sweet.

As the food was passed Mandy noticed Mrs. O'Laughlin took a generous portion of the ham biscuits, leaving only two for the boys to share. The girls politely ate bread and preserves without saying a word. When they finished, only a bit of the preserves remained but Mandy refused to worry. God had fed over 5,000 people with two loaves and a few fish. He could surely care for her little group.

With food in their stomachs the children sleepily washed and straggled off to bed, weary in body and mind. So many new experiences in one day had exhausted them and their adventure had just begun.

After Mandy had tucked the final child into bed with the usual hugs and kisses, she joined Mrs. O'Laughlin on the front porch. "Are there Yankee soldiers in the area now?" she asked, trying to get a feel for what she might encounter as they traveled.

"I haven't seen any for several months. They've taken just about everything from our fields and barns. There's nary a chicken or pig left within miles. We've nothing to give our own troops except what we can grow in a hurry or dig from the earth. Some of the farmers 'round about have taken to using bows and arrows to hunt wild game because by that method there is no tell-tale sound of a gun to alert the soldiers to our whereabouts," Mrs. O'Laughlin replied. "Our beautiful countryside is being destroyed. I'm not even sure we know what we are fighting for, or against. It's a travesty."

Mandy nodded. It was hard to believe the changes the war had brought; changes not only in the physical situations of people but changes in the heart and minds of a society once regarded as the politest and most cultivated in the nation. Well, she would continue to teach her children that God's goodness never fails regardless of the circumstances they came up against.

"I am so sorry you have had to endure such hardship," she said, smiling sadly at the distorted face of the older woman. "I pray the future will be kinder to you. Perhaps your son will return to you at the war's end. Don't give up hope." She patted Mrs. O'Laughlin's hand then sat quietly listening to the crickets singing in the bushes. As the moon rose over the pines, both women silently rose and went to bed.

After breakfast Mandy gathered her group together to outline the day's itinerary.

"Let us make a sincere effort to help Mrs. O'Laughlin with her chores before we leave this morning. Boys, you fill the woodbox and repair the broken shutter on the front window. Beth and Katie, straighten the upstairs. Lizzie, Susan and I will tidy the kitchen and wash windows. Neal, see if you can find something with which to grease that squeaky front door hinge. Please work quickly and carefully. I'd like to be ready to travel in two hours. Agreed?"

Everyone nodded soberly. They were as anxious as Mandy to continue their journey. It went without saying that if Mrs. O'Laughlin ate as much for dinner as she had the previous evening there would be precious little food left for the remainder of the trip.

Once on their way, they alternated walking, resting and nibbling. It was three o'clock before she heard the first complaint.

"My feet hurt," moaned Sam.

"So do mine," chorused Beth and John.

"Well, then, we'll take off our shoes and rest our feet," replied Mandy, looking for a grassy spot in the shade. "Here's the perfect place under this large pine tree. Wait. Let me spread a quilt so you won't stain your clothes. Who would like a drink? The water is warm but wet." Mandy passed the water jug from child to child making sure each drank several mouthfuls. Susan snuggled her cherubic face into Mandy's lap and was asleep in seconds. Her little legs had had all the walking they could take. Soon several of the others were napping on the quilt, their faces relaxed and serene. Mandy shooed the flies from them with a fallen pine branch. She felt relatively safe as they were only twelve miles from Columbia and the road was well traveled. To the casual passer-by they looked like a family on a picnic. Well, a picnic it would be. She opened her large valise and pulled out a loaf of bread and a jar of okra pickles. The food would give them all a burst of energy.

"Katie, please make us some sandwiches. One apiece except for Lizzie and Susan. Divide one in half for them. We'll rest for an hour then walk until the little ones give out." At four o'clock she woke those still sleeping, passed around the pickle sandwiches and ended the meal with some taffy she had been keeping for a special occasion.

"You don't have to wear your shoes if your feet still hurt. The road is soft and sandy. If you are careful where you step, you may walk barefooted," she said, smiling at the boys who eagerly stuffed their shoes in their valises. "See that farm house off in the distance? We'll go that far tonight. I'm sure the occupants will be glad to put us up. Let's sing a song, it will help to pass the time."

"In Dublin's fair city, where girls are so pretty," began

Katie, singing a favorite Irish ballad. Soon everyone was loudly chanting, "Singing cockles and mussels, alive, alive-o."

The farmhouse was farther away than it looked so Neal hoisted a tired Susan onto his back while Katie and Mandy took turns carrying Lizzie. By the time they reached the sandy wagon path to the farm everyone was footsore and sticky with sweat.

As they approached the house two yellow dogs, barking furiously, came bounding at them from around the shrubs causing the group to halt in their tracks.

"Stand still and they won't hurt you. Let them sniff your clothes. Perhaps they will sense we mean no harm. Sam! What are you doing?" Mandy held her breath as Sam, holding open his hand, boldly walk up the nearest dog.

"It's OK. They won't bite; their eyes are friendly. Squat down to their level and pet them. It scares a dog when someone hovers over him." Soon the dogs' tails were wagging a friendly welcome as they went from child to child licking fingers and sniffing pockets. With the crisis over, Mandy walked onto the front porch and knocked on the door. An ancient brown face with white curly hair appeared.

"Excuse me," Mandy said with a smile. "We were wondering if you would extend your hospitality to us and let us sleep in your barn tonight. We are on our way to Pendleton. It seems all the horses and carriages in Columbia were taken so we decided to walk until we could find another mode of transporta...."

"Sakes alive!" interrupted a thin, crackly voice. "How many chillins you got with you?"

"Eight."

" Mercy. You do beat all. The barn is too hot and stinky

but yer welcome to this porch. I have some straw mattresses you kin use." The door shut abruptly. After a few minutes an elderly black lady in a faded cotton dress made from flour sacks dragged three battered straw mattresses through the door opening. Next came several sheets worn so thin you could almost see through them. "Make yersef ta home." With that statement the door shut again.

Mandy added her linens to the bedding so everyone had some protection from the mosquitoes that buzzed around them incessantly, hungry for a tasty sip of blood. The children were so tired they fell asleep immediately without food or a wash-up. She was exhausted, too, but sleep evaded her so she sat against a porch pillar and tried to plan the next day's itinerary. Surely they would not be able to walk as far as they had today. Little legs were not used to such prolonged activity and Katie and Neal could not be expected to carry the little girls very far.

As she mulled over distances, the door opened and the lady, with an apologetic smile, offered Mandy a cup of herb tea. "It's bin a while since I've had company. De men folks is gone off fightin' or raidin' on their own. My garden was raided last fall and the last of my chickens stole. I manage to trap some rabbits and find wild greens and berries. I don't know what I'll do iffen the war stretches on much longer. Where did y'all say you were goin'? Are all dese chillin kin?" she asked in a husky whisper.

"We are on our way to Pendleton. I have friends there," Mandy replied, sipping the strong, bitter tea. "We came from Charleston where the war is intensifying. Do you know of any fighting near here? I would hate to lead the children into enemy territory."

"You'll be safe enuf. The war dun passed us by fer now.

Dis farm is a shadow of what it use ta be. Most of da black folk have either run off wid the Union army or headed north. Dis place oncet belong to white folk but they left a year ago. I was de cook. Now I'se gots a nice house if nuthin' else. Sorry I cain't help more." With a sigh the lady collected Mandy's empty cup and silently slipped back into the house.

Mandy turned her face to the star-studded heavens. "Oh Lord, please give us an easy day tomorrow. Send someone to help us. You are the God of miracles and we need a miracle, Lord. We need a miracle." With that plea uttered, she eased her weary body onto a corner of the mattress occupied by Katie and Beth, and slept.

A distant rumbling woke Mandy at dawn. Dark, angry clouds scuddled across the sky as lightening flashed and thunder grumbled. Suddenly the rain, driven by gusts of wind, began falling in sheets. Everyone woke and proceeded to drag the bedding to the inside porch wall. Mandy passed out the last of the bread, jam and dried fruit which disappeared in seconds.

"It seems we will have to put off our journey for a while this morning," she said. "I imagine this storm won't last too long. Rain before seven, clear before eleven, they say. When the lightening stops, you may go out in the wet if you care to. It may be the only bath you get for a while. We'll use one of the light blankets as a towel." It didn't take much coaxing to get the boys into the rain. They found a round stone and began to play catch and keep away. Soon the girls joined in. In a few minutes they all looked like drowned rats with their hair hanging in sodden hanks and their wet clothes sticking to their bodies. Mandy wet a rag and washed her hands and face deciding she would find a better situation in which to bathe.

The storm ended as abruptly as it had begun. A watery

sun peeked through misty clouds promising another hot, humid day.

"Well, now the road won't be so dusty," said the old lady, as they helped her with the mattresses. After voicing their thanks the bedraggled group began their walk with renewed enthusiasm. The rain had been a blessing in disguise.

Soon the countryside began to dip and roll, leaving the little ones breathless. Mandy decided for every hour of walking they did, they would stop for a fifteen-minute rest. It was during the second rest period as she struggled to pull a thorn from John's foot that she heard the rattle of wagon wheels coming up behind them. She searched in vain for cover but there was none to be found so they gathered together and stood at anxious attention as an ancient, bony, lop-eared mule came over the rise pulling a farm wagon filled with milk cans. Driving the wagon was a scarecrow of a man, wearing a battered straw hat and patched work clothes.

"Afternoon, Miss," he said, tipping his hat. "Out for a bit of a walk or visiting a neighbor?"

"We're going to Pendleton," piped Lizzie before Mandy could hush her.

"Pendleton, is it? That's a mighty long walk for little legs like yours. Tell you what, if your mama doesn't mind a few stops along the way, you young ones can ride in the wagon. Caesar won't mind a bit of extra weight." Then, looking at Mandy, he explained, "I've got several more milk deliveries to make, but I'm going in the general direction of Pendleton. Clyde Pepper's my name."

Mandy carefully searched his ancient, wrinkled face and decided he looked honest. "It would be a great blessing for the youngsters to ride a while. May we put our valises in the wagon also?"

"Sure 'nough. Use that old quilt to sit on, ladies, so as not to get splinters in your bottoms." Mr. Pepper pulled some of the milk cans toward the front of the wagon to make more room for the luggage.

Beth giggled at his speech as she spread out the worn quilt which normally was wrapped around the full milk cans to keep them cool, then helped Susan and Lizzie find a comfortable spot.

"Here's the place for you, young man," Mr. Pepper said, looking at Sam and patting the seat next to him. "You learn to drive ol' Caesar, here, to give me a rest."

Sam clambered up the wagon wheel and plopped on the seat, his face aglow at the prospect of driving the mule.

"Hold the reins just so. Careful, don't pull on his mouth. That's better. Giddap, Caesar." The aged animal leaned into its neck collar and the wagon began to roll along slowly.

"Caesar could do this route without me, I reckon, since we've been carting milk for nigh on to twenty years over the same roads. Only, now with the war an' all, not many folks can pay much but still I trade for a bit of meat or vegetables when I can. Truth be told, it's hard to find enough food to hold body and soul together. I've managed to keep three cows and a bull calf hidden so I still have milk to sell. The rest of the herd was 'donated' to the army one night. Seems soldiers on both sides just take what they need without askin'. Mighty impolite, to my way 'o thinkin'."

Mandy nodded sympathetically as she and the older children walked beside the wagon. A cloud of gnats buzzed around their eyes, but shooing them away took too much energy. After about twenty minutes, the milkman turned onto a neglected wagon path. The only indication of a farm was a dilapidated wooden fence that ran back into a pine grove.

"No use you folks walking extra. Y'all set down in this here grass whilst I take the milk to the house. Be back shortly." Mr. Pepper took the reins from Sam.

Mandy helped the girls from the wagon. Sam, in a fit of vanity, jumped from the driver's seat, landing on one knee. "Miss Mandy, I'm hungry. My innards are growling," he complained, holding his hand on his stomach.

"There's not much left to eat, so chew each piece a long time," cautioned Mandy as she passed out the last bits of bread left over from breakfast. "Drink a lot of water. It will help fill you up. From now on we will have to find our dinner before we can eat. Keep your eyes open for berries and greens. Neal and John will have to sharpen their hunting skills, but don't worry, the Lord will provide."

The rattle of milk cans announced the return of Mr. Pepper. As the children clambered aboard he held up a woven reed basket. "Look what I've got," he chortled, gleefully. "Dew berries, fresh picked. Help yerself." The words were hardly out of his mouth before eight pairs of hands eagerly reached for the glistening black berries that were devoured in minutes, leaving behind purple stained fingers and lips as the only evidence of their existence.

"Yum! Where did those berries come from? Can we get more?" asked John.

"You kin find them in fields and 'long side the roads. Keep yer eyes open whilst yer walkin'. We had a wet spring so berries are plentiful this year. Those were all the lady had to trade me for milk."

"Oh, dear! I'm afraid the children ate your supper!" exclaimed Mandy.

"Oh posh. An old man like me doesn't need much feedin'. Now iffen y'all had a wad of chawin' tobaccy I'd be much obliged. But then y'all don't seem the type to chew an' spit." Mr. Pepper's thin voice crackled as he chuckled at his joke.

Mandy laughed, too. His light-hearted nature relaxed the tension she felt being provider and protector of eight little people.

After the final delivery, Caesar ambled down an open field. As they neared a stand of pines, Mandy could see a ramshackle wooden barn half hidden by wild bushes and brambles.

"It's too late to go much farther today," said Mr. Pepper. "You folks just make yerselves comfortable in the barn. Don't light any fires though as I've got the cows hid and don't want to draw attention to this place. People think the farm is deserted and that's the way I want it."

Mandy understood. Survival meant devious strategies these days. Quietly the children spread their blankets, filled their tummies with fresh, warm milk compliments of a cow named Daisy and drifted into slumber.

A rosy light was outlining the tall pines against the pre-dawn sky when Mandy heard the muffled creaking of the old farm wagon. Hurriedly she walked to the edge of the path where she could talk to Mr. Pepper without waking the children. She wanted to ask if she could hire him to take them to Pendleton. It would be worth every cent she had to get to safety as soon as possible.

"I've just finished the milkin' and thought I'd let your brood drink their fill before beginning my rounds," he said, halting Caesar and lifting a large bucket topped with creamy white froth from the wagon. "I'm afraid there's little to go with it except a bit of corn meal. We could stir it in if that would help."

"Thank you so much for thinking of us," replied Mandy, sincerely. Then getting right to the point, she said, "I know it would be an imposition but could you take us all the way to Pendleton? I would be glad to pay you for your services."

"I'm afraid that would be impossible, much as I wish I could. It's the cows; they need milking twice a day in order to keep them producing enough milk for my business. I've no one to ask to take over whilst I'm gone, don't you see."

"Oh. I didn't think of that. You're right, of course. Well, it was just a thought." Mandy swallowed her disappointment. "I'll wake the children and hurry them along so as not to delay you." The promise of fresh milk brought everyone from their hay beds without a grumble. Even without cooking, the corn meal, mixed in the milk to make a mush, was consumed in record time. While they feasted, Mr. Pepper entertained them with stories about Caesar in his younger days.

"Twarn't a door he couldn't open or a gate latch he couldn't undo. Land sakes, I was hard pressed to keep the grain somewhere he couldn't reach. Mostly I hoisted it to a makeshift ledge near the top of the barn. I swear one day I saw him studyin' the rope and pulley, tryin' to figure out how to get his own supper. He shor 'nuff liked the company of lady mules, too. Every time he got loose he went callin' at a mule farm down the road. There he'd stand outside the pasture just a brayin' til his favorite gals came to the fence to say 'howdy'. I declare I was glad when the old boy turned twenty and gave up his wily ways."

"Twenty!" gasped Sam. "How old is Caesar now?"

"Wal, let's see. He was twenty the year before the war begun..." Mr. Pepper counted on his fingers. "Guess that makes him about twenty-four, give or take a little. Never had a sick day in his life, neither. He's been my closest friend since my wife passed ten year ago. We're plannin' on goin' out together. Life just wouldn't be the same without the ol' boy."

"Now, iffen you youngsters are ready to travel, I'll take you several miles in yer direction. Got some milk customers that-a-way so's it'd be no trouble."

"Can I steer Caesar like I did yesterday?" asked Sam, eagerly.

"Don't see why not. Caesar seems agreeable. That's what counts."

With the smaller children again riding in the wagon, they began the day's trek. Although the old mule ambled along slower than they would have walked, little legs were getting a rest and they were still moving toward their destination.

"This is as far as I go," stated the old gentleman, several hours later. "You're on your own from here. But look, there's a big patch of dew berries right 'long side the road. Better pick 'em before someone else does. Poke a stick in there first just in case there's a snake snoozin' in the shade. Miss Mandy, if you sleep in the open, find a hidey hole. There's been a Yankee scout come through here off an' on."

Mandy extended her hand to Mr. Pepper. "We are very much obliged for all your kindness. God bless you."

"Perhaps we'll meet again under better circumstances. Been real nice havin' yer company." He tipped his sweat-stained hat, clucked to his mule and turned down a weedy driveway.

"Better pick the berries. They may have to do for your lunch. Katie, put them in this satchel where I had the food. It still has its wax paper lining. Boys, let Susan and Lizzie pick the easiest spots. You climb up a bit and get those big ones in the middle."

For the next half an hour little fingers suffered thorny pricks as they harvested the shiny, purple-black globes. Most of the berries went from hand to mouth but when they had picked the patch clean the satchel held about two quarts for their supper.

The day progressed in an orderly fashion: walk until the children grew weary, then rest until they were ready to continue. Determined to keep their minds as active as their bodies, Mandy gave them arithmetic problems to solve in their heads or quizzed them on historical events. She taught them as many survival techniques as she could remember, making sure Katie and Neal understood all emergency procedures.

By late afternoon everyone was more than ready to set up camp. Since they were in an isolated area of pines and oaks, Mandy decided to forage for wild mushrooms and greens while the children rested. It wasn't long before her small basket began to fill. Suddenly she spotted a honeybee laden with pollen. Eagerly she followed it toward the community hive in a hollow tree. A dark stain dribbled from a crack in the trunk assuring her that sweet riches lay inside. Quickly she lined a corner of her basket with leaves and, covering as much of her face and arms as she could with a leafy branch, she gently reached into the tree cavity and withdrew a large chunk of honeycomb dripping with golden honey. Although the bees buzzed nervously around her, they did not attack. Twice more she raided the hive before the bees lost patience with her. Now their droning reached a higher frequency as they began to circle her angrily.

"All right. I'm leaving. Thank you for the gift of honey. You have helped us immensely." Mandy spoke softly, while slowly backing away from the tree. The bees followed her for a few hundred feet but she received no stings. When they returned to their hive she hurried toward camp.

"That was mighty brave, ma'am, robbing a bee tree without a smoking torch," said a deep voice. Mandy whirled around in terror. Half hidden by the trunk of a huge white oak was a soldier, dressed in buckskin, a Union army cap shading his eyes. He sat easily astride a large bay horse. Mandy froze. To run would be foolish. She must try to lead him away from the children. She stared at his craggy face, trying to read his intentions.

"It's all right. Our war is not with young women, especially pretty women like you. I've been raised to be a gentleman." The soldier's face broke into an engaging smile as he doffed his hat revealing wavy, blond locks tied back along his neck. His bright blue eyes looked at her with compassion as if understanding her situation. Slowly he reached around his saddle, then tossed a furry bundle at her feet causing her to jump back in fear before she recognized the bodies of several grey squirrels.

"Hope this will help a little," he said. "Those children look mighty hungry." Before Mandy could utter a word, he spurred his horse and disappeared into the shadows.

"Well, I declare. Lord, I'm not sure whether I just saw an angel or a Yankee, but thank You very much for supper." She snatched up the squirrels and hurried back to camp thinking, the soldier knew about the children, did the children know about him?

By the time she returned, the boys had gathered enough wood to last the night, Katie had a pot of water simmering on the fire, Neal had cut pine boughs for bedding that Alex had piled in two separate locations. The rest of the children were washing their faces and hands with a wet towel.

"Miss Mandy! Where did you get those squirrels?" asked John, who had unsuccessfully tried to trap a rabbit.

"Let's just say God provided," Mandy replied with a smile, giving them to Neal to skin. "Look what else I found: honey!

We'll have a feast tonight."

The discovery of the honey cancelled any further inquiry about the squirrels. Mandy passed around chunks of honey in the comb. Chewing the delectable sweet put everyone in a happy mood. This was a fine adventure.

Chapter Four

Slowly but surely they were putting the miles behind them. Each day was broken into definite segments: search for food, walk and rest. By the eighth day even Susan and Lizzie had toughened to the point of walking for several hours without complaining. Occasionally people on horseback or in buggies passed them, but rarely was there a wagon large enough to hold all nine of them, and the vehicles that could were driven by rough looking men who intimidated Mandy. She felt safer on her own.

Neal was the restless one. At fourteen, he had little patience for the snail's pace of travel. "Please, Miss Mandy, let me go on ahead. I can get to Pendleton and send a wagon back for you," he pleaded again and again.

"It's too dangerous, Neal. The Yankee soldiers would take you for a spy or deserter. You never know where or when they'll turn up. Besides, you are the oldest. We need your hunting skills. You are the only one who can trap rabbits. John is too clumsy and Sam doesn't have the heart for it," stated Mandy, firmly.

"I don't believe there are any soldiers around here. By now they're all fighting in Charleston. Will they destroy St. Phillips or our house? I hope they don't find the silver. You should let me join the army. I'd show those blue coats a thing or two." Neal scuffed the dusty road with his bare foot to emphasize his words.

Mandy sighed. "I'm sure you would, Neal. Just be patient. Once we get to Pendleton there will be excitement and challenge aplenty, even for you. Now please carry Susan for a while. She is beginning to stagger a bit."

It was an exceptionally hot, humid day. Dark, low hanging clouds drifted across the sky and the smell of rain was in the air. Suddenly the wind began to gust, twisting the trees to and fro. Mandy could hear the low rumble of thunder off in the distance.

"Boys, run ahead and see if you can find some shelter for us. I think we are in for a storm." Mandy's words were lost in the wind as soon as she spoke them. She grabbed Susan's and Lizzie's hands to steady them while the wind whipped their clothes so violently she felt like a sheet on a clothesline in a hurricane.

"Over here!" shouted Neal, waving and pointing to the left where a small, three-sided shed nestled under several towering oaks. In bygone days it had no doubt been a shelter for pasture animals. Stumbling over fallen branches and dodging briars that threatened to snag their clothing, they hurried to cover just as a driving rain pelted down from angry looking thunderheads. Mandy ordered everyone to snuggle in the corners to stay as dry as possible.

Overhead the trees groaned as the wind contorted their limbs. She could hear the crash of branches as they tore loose from their source. Then the sky turned dark and had an unusual eerie, green glow that seemed to turn everything a dirty yellow hue. The wind stopped for a moment as if in anticipation of the ghastly devastation to come.

Now came the most terrifying sound of all: a low, constant roar, not unlike that of a train engine straining uphill. Mandy put her arms around her wards to shield them as the top half of a mighty oak splintered and smashed into the ground in front of them with an earth shaking crash. Susan and Lizzie screamed with fright and buried their faces in Mandy's skirt while Katie and Neal clung to Alex and Beth. The swirling air was filled with dust and sand making it almost impossible to breathe. Tall pine trees snapped like matchsticks littering the woods with green branches. Mighty oaks were torn from the ground as if plucked by a giant hand. For a few seconds the roar overwhelmed their senses, reaching the very depths of their beings as the ground itself trembled in fear. Then, as quickly as it had come, the storm ended, leaving behind the sound of rain dripping from the remaining trees and a gentle, almost apologetic, breeze.

"Is it over?" quavered Alex, who had buried his head under his arms. Lizzie and Susan refused to budge, pinning Mandy against the shed.

"Miss Mandy, I don't feel so good," whimpered John. "My leg hurts."

Mandy disentangled herself from the girls and crawled to the corner of the shed where John was wedged in by part of the fallen oak. After breaking away some of the smaller limbs, she saw his leg was pinned beneath the weight of a large branch.

"Neal, Katie, Sam, help me lift this branch off John's leg. John, when you feel the weight shift, pull your leg free quickly.

I don't know how long we can hold up the tree. Sam, over there; Katie, watch that broken branch, don't let it stab John as we lift; Neal, help me on the heavy end. Ready? On three. One, two, three!"

Groaning with the effort, the four managed to rock the heavy branch up enough for John to free his leg. Fortunately, it wasn't broken but there were several deep gashes where shattered limbs had scraped his leg on impact. Mandy carefully wiped the bloody abrasions with a clean cloth and applied a salve to prevent infection. Thankfully, he was the only physical casualty; mentally they were all feeling a bit rocky.

"This shelter is the safest place for us tonight. I'm afraid more trees may fall and it will be very difficult to see our way over the debris in this half-light. Who would like something to eat? I've a bit more honey. Wipe your hands on your wet clothing. Tomorrow I'll wash everything so we will be clean when we reach Pendleton. It can't be far now." Mandy hoped saying the words would bring them to pass.

"I know, let's play scripture find. I'll go first. These words are from a verse in Psalms: refuge, strength, trouble." Katie attempted to divert everyone's attention.

"That's easy," said Neal. "God is our refuge and strength, a very present help in trouble. He helped us just now to find shelter and kept us safe from the storm, except for John, but, really, John isn't hurt very badly. I think the words come from Psalm forty-nine."

"Right you are, Neal, Psalm forty-nine, verse one. Here is another, this time from Proverbs: trust, lean, understanding." Katie immediately responded.

"I know," exclaimed Sam, quickly. "Trust in the Lord with all thine heart; and lean not unto thine own understanding. Proverbs three, five."

"Very good, Sam. What a lively mind you have. Who can apply that verse to our situation?" Mandy's challenge set minds busily thinking.

"If we had stayed in Charleston like we wanted to maybe something bad would have happened so God told us to go to Pendleton and we are trusting Him to get us there safely. Does that sound right?" John looked at Mandy, wistfully. "I just wish God would have made our trip a little easier. If we are in His will, why is our trip so hard and take so long?" The throbbing of his injured leg created his negative response.

"Perhaps God is testing our faith," she suggested. "If we are faithful to Him in this situation, He will trust us with even greater adventures. Remember, God tests our strengths, not our weaknesses. He already knows we will not fail, and we won't. Here's another one from Proverbs that we can apply to today: death, life, tongue."

"I think I can say it right," said Katie. "'Death and life are in the power of the tongue: and they that love it shall eat the fruit thereof.' Proverbs eighteen, twenty-one. That means we are what we say. If we say this journey is too hard and we will never get there, we might give up and go back, only to face a worse situation. Sometimes, if we keep repeating something about ourselves such as 'I'm shy' or 'I'm stubborn', we begin to believe it even if it's not true, and start acting that way."

"I have one," interrupted Beth. "Mouth, tongue, troubles."

"I give up," laughed Mandy, after a few seconds of silence. "Nobody seems to know that verse. Tell us, please."

"It's from Proverbs Twenty-one, verse twenty-three. 'Whoso keepeth his mouth and his tongue keepeth his soul from troubles.' I read that verse last month and memorized it to remind me not to say whatever silly thing pops into my head. I'm trying to think before I speak." Beth grinned as

Katie laughed in unbelief.

"Good idea, Beth. Words can get us into a lot of trouble if we aren't careful. When I was a little girl my mother taught me this saying: 'If you can't say something nice, don't say anything at all.' That is good advice for everyone." Mandy's sober look hushed Katie's teasing.

The rest of the afternoon she spent trying to keep up their spirits by telling stories- the funnier the better, and playing geography games. Finally, one by one they drifted to sleep, cuddling close to each other to ward off the damp night air. But it was an uneasy rest for Susan, who woke several times in tears, her overactive mind reliving the terror of the tornado. The night was almost gone before Mandy relaxed enough to sleep. In addition to her concern for John's leg, she was desperately hungry.

When Mandy finally awoke the morning sun's rays had already begun burning away the misty haze. To her delight Neal had crept away at dawn and caught a rabbit that was now roasting on a makeshift spit and Katie was boiling water for Indian coffee. John was peeling the bark from a branch Sam had found that was shaped like a crutch.

"I've saved some English tea in case of an emergency," said Mandy, digging into her personal valise. "Today is as much of an emergency as I need to use them."

They sat contently around the fire sipping tea and chewing on the well done but tough rabbit parts. Mandy encouraged them to talk about the tornado and to express their fears. "There is no shame in being afraid. We all fear something, sometime. Courage is learning to function wisely in the face of fear. Don't let fear rob you of your common sense. You have done very well under the circumstances. I'm proud of you all. Now, let's put out the fire and walk carefully away from this jumble of fallen branches and trees. Once in the clear we will change clothes and hold a laundry day. Those not doing domestic chores can forage for food."

It took several hours of climbing over fallen timber, hoisting Susan and Lizzie over logs too large to climb, and avoiding flooded areas before they again reached a clear section of the road. After another lengthy walk they chanced upon a meadow containing a small pond.

"Here's the perfect spot for doing the laundry," said Mandy. "The sun will dry your clothes quickly. Girls, wrap yourselves in blankets and let me have everything you are wearing. Boys, you set a few traps and hunt for greens and berries. When I've finished with the girls' clothes, I'll call you."

The morning was successful in all endeavors. The clothes were washed and dried and a fat woodchuck whose leg had been injured in the storm became the main ingredient of a delicious stew that energized everyone.

Because of John's injury, the afternoon's walk was slower than usual. He staggered along silently, aided by the forked branch that served as a crutch, but his set jaw and ashen face revealed his pain. As they rounded a bend in the road, Mandy's heart raced as she recognized the large farmhouse on a knoll set amidst pecan trees. The Gibbes had stopped here. This family was quite prosperous and had several girls her age.

"Katie, Neal, take everyone over to that stone wall and rest. I am going to see if we will be welcome at that farm. I'll be back in a few minutes." Mandy hurried up the red clay driveway and knocked boldly but politely on the weathered front door. The door opened, revealing an elderly lady in a worn floral dress and white eyelet apron. Mandy recognized her at once.

"Mrs. Reed? I'm Mandy Greene. I stayed with you years ago when the Gibbes and Stewarts stopped here on their way to Beaufort. Do you remember me?"

The lady looked at her carefully. "I vaguely recall the visit. Seems you were quite shy at the time and spent most of the time in your room, reading. How is Nana Stewart? I've had only two letters from them since they were here. Lord, have mercy! I'm forgetting my manners. Won't you come in and sit a spell? However did you get here? Where is your buggy?"

"Mrs. Reed, I've a favor to ask. I'm now the mistress of a small orphanage – only eight precious children – and most of them half-grown. We are on our way to Pendleton and need accommodations for the night. Could we stay here? We'd be no bother. The barn will be fine. We're used to camping out."

"Eight children? I swan! Bring them to the house. It's been years since I've had a passel of youngsters here so it will be a real treat! I'll start cooking." With an eager smile Mrs. Reed flung open the door then trotted toward the kitchen.

Mandy hurried down the lane to where the children could see her and waved them toward the house. Soon the kitchen was filled with childish chatter as Susan and Lizzie played with old cornhusk dolls and Alex and Sam inspected a new batch of kittens under the back porch. Neal piled wood neatly in a rack near the stove while Beth and Katie set a long trestle table with fine china taken from a trunk hidden in the root cellar. John, unable to participate, rested his injured leg on a stool and watched.

"You young folk can wash up in the mud room. Feel free to wash your hair or whatever. There's extra towels in the chest under the window," said their hostess, her face flushed from the heat of the stove. With one hand she mixed a batch of buttermilk biscuits, with the other she sauteed deer meat with cabbage and onions.

"Life is not as it was," she said to Mandy. "My husband's business closed when the supply ships could not get through so he joined the army. My daughters both married well but live on plantations a two days drive from here. They used to visit quite often but now traveling is dangerous and they both have small children to tend. I confess to being a bit lonely. These young voices are music to my ears." She opened a jar of chow-chow and another of watermelon pickles.

"Food is scarce but my husband had me stash a large supply from his store before the supplies dwindled. I've managed to keep a productive garden behind the wood lot and I dry as much as I can. Fortunately, a neighbor killed a doe last week and gave me a roast. There's just enough left to make a good gravy."

After placing a steaming cup of peppermint tea in Mandy's hand, Mrs. Reed bustled back and forth seasoning this and stirring that. Soon the kitchen filled with savory smells. Susan, putting aside her doll, marched boldly up to the harried cook, pulled on her apron and announced, "I'm hungry, please."

"Bless you, child. Here's some bread and jam to take the edge off your hunger. Dinner will be ready in an hour." She pulled a fresh loaf of bread from the cupboard and deftly cut eight thick slices. Everyone lined up behind Susan to partake of the treat. The rapt look on their faces as they chewed spoke volumes about the stress of their journey. Mandy's heart ached as she realized the extent of their deprivation.

She leaned against the cane backing of the chair and was surprised to feel her legs trembling and tears flooding her eyes. The strain of keeping up a brave front was taking its toll. Suddenly she felt bone weary. The heat from the woodstove made her drowsy. Excusing herself, she moved to the back porch where a soft breeze cooled her heated brow. Bracing herself against a post, she closed her eyes and napped, heedless of the commotion.

The next thing she knew Katie was shaking her. "Mrs. Reed says dinner is ready but she won't let us eat until you join us." Mandy shook the cobwebs from her brain, rose unsteadily and went to the mudroom to wash. The cool spring water was refreshing and she realized she was ravenous.

"My! That looks good! What a blessing to feast on real home cooked food. Children, lets give thanks." Mandy stood beside her chair as eight heads bowed. "Heavenly Father, thank You for a safe journey, for Mrs. Reed's hospitality, and this good food. Help us to be mindful of others and to serve You with a joyful heart. Amen."

There was a sudden clatter of china as platters of greens, gravy, and biscuits were quickly passed. A comfortable silence prevailed as they concentrated on filling their stomachs. Even Susan, the picky eater, cleaned her plate and asked for seconds.

"What a wonderful meal! We can't thank you enough." Mandy looked around the table at smiling faces. "Mrs. Reed, you must let us try to repay you a little by doing some needful chores tomorrow. The boys are strong and willing and the girls are very good helpers. You make a list and we'll all work together to see everything gets done. Right now I know two little girls who are ready for bed." She recognized the drowsy expression on Susan's and Lizzie's faces.

"I opened the windows upstairs. Put the girls in the large front bedroom. I have extra eiderdown mattresses the boys can use. Save the west room for them. You take the small back room. The linens are in the cedar chest. I'll sleep down here on the settee. No protesting. I often sleep there when I'm restless. There's a pot of hot water on the stove if anyone needs it." Mrs. Reed smiled as she gathered an armful of dirty dishes and bustled to the kitchen.

"Katie, would you and Beth please help clean up while I get these sleepyheads to bed? Since we all bathed this morning in the pond, I'll just sponge them off tonight." Mandy filled a basin with warm water, found a wash cloth and towel and ushered the girls up the back stairs to their room. As she dried their feet, playing a game with their toes, Mrs. Reed appeared with several cotton nightgowns.

"Try these for size. The girls will sleep better if they are comfortable. I've been saving these gowns for my granddaughters but so far all the grandchildren are boys."

The cotton batiste felt like silk to Mandy as she pulled the gowns over the girls' heads. The soft, light cloth reminded her of a more civilized era when fine, fashionable clothes were the norm and dinner tables were laden with the most succulent of menus. Then men and women chatted amicably about the most recently read books or listened to music played skillfully on the pianoforte or violin. Mandy remembered how awed she had been at the everyday opulence of the Gibbes: closets full of gowns, two or three meats at every meal. Then she chided herself; life was more than fancy clothes and fine food. Change happened. One could bend with the winds of time or snap. Right now she was learning to bend. It was character building. She laid the extra nightgowns on a ladder back chair for Katie and Beth then took the wash water downstairs to empty.

The girls had worked wonders in the kitchen. The dishes were washed and put away, the table wiped clean and the floor swept. Mandy flashed them a look of gratitude saying,

"Mrs. Reed has an extensive library. If you ask, I'm sure she won't mind if you select a book to read."

Katie's eyes brightened at the thought of fresh reading material. They rushed to the parlor where Mrs. Reed was placing bed linens on the settee. "Mrs. Reed, Miss Mandy suggested we ask you if we could read some of your books. We'll be very careful with them," said Katie, unable to hide the excitement in her voice.

"Land sakes, just help yourself. My husband and girls are avid readers. The library is opposite this room across the hall. Take what you like."

The girls scampered into the library and gazed hungrily at the rows of books lining the walls. They had never seen so many in one place before. "How will we know what to choose?" asked Beth, in an awestruck whisper.

"Read the titles. When you find something that sounds interesting, take it down and see if you can read it," explained Katie. "Some of these are law books and biographies of famous persons. Look! Here are the writings of Thomas Payne. This book about agriculture is by Thomas Jefferson. Mr. Reed must be a very rich and important man to have such books," said Katie, reverently.

Just then Mrs. Reed bustled into the room. "Need a little help? I forgot to tell you the books our girls enjoyed at your age are over here in this corner. Of course, you are welcome to read anything, but these may be of more interest."

Beth hurried to where Mrs. Reed pointed. She studied the titles for a while then chose a story about Pocahontas. Katie remained where she was just reading titles. She noticed everything was categorized by topic: law, religion, agriculture, social concerns, etc. Finally she selected a book entitled Famous Speeches of the Continental Congress.

While Beth read of the early life of the New England Settlements, Katie found herself transported to a meeting of the Continental Congress where John Adams boldly declared:

"Before God, I believe the hour has come. My judgment approves this matter, and my whole heart is in it. All that I have and all that I am, and all that I hope in this life, I am now ready here to stake upon it. And as I leave off as I began, that live or die, survive or perish, I am for the Declaration (of Independence). It is my living sentiment and by the blessing of God it shall be my dying sentiment. Independence now, and independence forever!"

Closing her eyes she let her thoughts dwell on the words: "independence forever". Was that what this war was all about? Surely a nation with such fervent idealistic men who pledged their all to gain freedom from British tyranny should somehow expect everyone, regardless of nationality or religion, to enjoy the freedom they had fought so hard to gain.

A sudden fear invaded her thoughts. What if the South won the war and the country was divided into two or more parts. Would a stronger nation prey on the weakness of the divided States and attempt a takeover? Might she someday be a citizen of France, Spain or England? She shuddered at the thought. Then rousing herself from the prospect of such dire events she turned the page and saw a quote from Benjamin Franklin.

"I have lived, Sir, a long time, and the longer I live, the more convincing proofs I see of this truth – that God governs in the affairs of men. And if a sparrow cannot fall to the ground without His notice, is it probable that an empire can rise without His aid?

I have been assured, Sir, in the Sacred Writings, that 'except the Lord build the house, they labor in vain that build it.' I firmly believe this; and I also believe that without His concurring aid we shall succeed in this political building no better than the builders of Babel: we shall be divided by our partial local interests; our projects will be confounded, and we ourselves shall become a reproach and bye word down to future ages."

So, even Mr. Franklin feared a foreign invasion if the states did not form a solid union. Had Jeff Davis and the other Southern aristocrats thought of the ruin they would bring upon this country by dividing it? Many souls had died already to preserve its precious freedom! Should these men have died in vain?

"O God," she prayed, desperately, "You built this nation on Christian principals and freedoms that allow each person to express his individuality. You do not care what color a person's skin is for You created people of all colors. Please don't let us be divided. Let this war end in such a way that this country's godly principals will be preserved. Save us, Lord, save us. Amen." Sobered by what she had read, she carefully placed the book back in its place and left the room.

"Why, Katie, whatever is the matter? Why the long face? I thought you were enjoying reading," said Mandy, encountering her in the hallway.

"The book I was reading made me think seriously about this war. Miss Mandy, do you think God wants us to fight? What will happen if the South wins? Will we be divided from the North? Is slavery right? If not, who would work the plantations?

"Goodness! Such deep thoughts from such a pretty head," replied Mandy, delaying a reply while she formulated her thoughts.

"Personally, I do not approve of one person owning another. It is degrading and a vicious type of control. Some people do not even regard the Negro as the same human species as white people, which I find ridiculous. God created us all and Jesus died for the sins of the whole world regardless of our race or beliefs. I am sure God does not approve of war, even though He used it to discipline the children of Israel and other nations written about in the Old Testament. However, I believe God is guiding this country because our founders strived to include His laws in our constitution. Perhaps this war is His purifying effort, to make us a stronger, more holy nation. All we can do is pray that His will be done and that righteousness prevail."

"I don't think I want to live in the South any longer," Katie said in a shaky voice.

"Not all Southerners believe in slavery, Katie. Many good Christian folk here have never used slaves. What the South needs is more farm machinery to take the place of human labor. Your way of thinking will help heal us once the war is over. Your generation will be the one, hopefully, to give us the inventions we need. Don't give up. Hold on to what is good. The best is yet to come." Mandy smiled as she smoothed Katie's hair in an effort to comfort her. Here was a girl on the verge of womanhood who was questioning social customs and seeking higher ideals. Did she realize the power one person had to sway a nation toward good or evil?

"Miss Mandy! Sam won't let me help stack wood. I can do it! Tell him to let me help." Alex's plaintive cry came from the mudroom. Giving Katie a quick hug, Mandy hurried to resolve another minor incident. At least Alex was willing to help. She would have him load the kindling into a large bucket. There was plenty of work to go around.

Chapter Five

Saying good-by to Mrs. Reed was difficult. She represented shelter and hospitality. However, Mandy was determined to press on. At least they could travel comfortably as the generous woman had given them enough provisions for several days. On the tenth day of their trek, as they passed an abandoned shed in a pine grove near the road, a black man stepped out from the shadows.

"Miss Mandy? It's Toby. 'Member me? I dun worked for Mista Adger when you was der."

"Toby! Oh Toby! A familiar face at last! Are we near Pendleton? I was tempted to ask the few travelers we met on the road yesterday, but I didn't want to seem as if I was lost." Mandy's heart beat joyfully at the sight of an old friend.

"Yo letter come two days ago. Mista Smith tol me to wait fo y'all by the road. The Yankee soldiers bin pesterin' us some. Mista Smith tol me to let him know when I sees you. He'll come wid de buggy to fetch you. Youse is to stay by dis here shed an' wait. Stay otta sight and be quiet as church mice.

I'se a runner 'tween plantations. I specs I'll be home 'fo dark tomorrow. I'se on my way." With those brief instructions, he disappeared into the underbrush.

"Well, you heard him. Let's camp by the shed, away from the road. By this time day after tomorrow we'll be home. Quietly, now, we don't want to attract any attention." Mandy could hardly disguise her disappointment. The Union soldiers were here, too. Like bad pennies, they were turning up everywhere. Strange, they had not encountered any soldiers on the road and she had not heard any gunshots or canon fire. Perhaps the situation was not as threatening as in Charleston. With a sigh she dropped to the ground unloading the cumbersome valise and water jugs she had been carrying.

"Why don't we try to nap since we may be traveling at night? Neal and John, you will have to be lookouts after dark so try to catch some winks now. Hopefully, you won't fall asleep later." She spread a quilt for them under the shade of the pines, tossing a few stray pinecones to one side.

While they slept, the others played cats-in-the-cradle, mumbly peg, or chained weeds all with a minimum of noise. After supper, the boys crept into some bushes by the edge of the road to watch for unwelcome intruders or soldiers.

A thin sliver of a new moon rose but the scant light it offered was consumed by shadows that were dark and deep. Neal kept John awake by telling horror stories but he scared John so badly talking about a blood-thirsty panther that they decided to think of other entertainment. Then the hoof beats of horses, mixed with the creak of wagon wheels, was heard. It was a regiment of Union soldiers. The boys flattened themselves to the ground and held their breath as the troops passed by, moving like a ghostly apparition in the night; the only noise the gentle snorting of the horses. After what seemed an eternity, the last artillery wagon, towing a large cannon, rolled out of sight.

"Wow!" whispered Neal. "No wonder the Yankees are winning! Did you see the size of that cannon? It could blow up a whole town!"

"Do you think there are more soldiers coming? Maybe we should hide farther in the woods," said John, anxiously.

"We're supposed to be on guard, John, not running away. Those soldiers didn't see us so others won't either. The trick is to blend in with the scenery. Lay low and don't move. If more soldiers come, we'll count them and note their supplies. Perhaps we can be of use as spies." Neal was really getting into the game. This was more fun than soldiering. They sat quietly for the remainder of the night but saw nothing more exciting than a fox stalking a rabbit. As the sky lightened they crept from their lair and hurried to the shed.

"Miss Mandy! We saw some Yankee soldiers with all sorts of guns and a big cannon. They didn't see us. Neal wasn't even afraid," John reported, breathless from reliving the scene.

"They might have been the soldiers who were bothering the folks at Pendleton," stated Neal, matter-of-factly. "They were headed toward Columbia. Must have been at least fifty or sixty of them."

"Oh, dear. I put you boys right in danger's way," fretted Mandy. "Perhaps I should take the night watch tonight."

"This is a job for men, not ladies," boasted Neal. "Don't worry. We know what to do. They didn't see us and no one else will, either."

"All right. I trust your instincts. Besides God has protected us thus far and we only have one more night to go. Now, have breakfast then try to get some sleep." Mandy passed a box of biscuits in their direction, along with a water bottle and some dried apples. If she could just keep the children quietly occupied for one more day their journey would be over.

"Let's look as presentable as possible to the people of Pendleton," she said, digging into her valise for her leather sewing pouch. "Beth, you and Katie try to mend the rips in Lizzie's and Susan's dresses. I'll do the boys shirts and pants. Here is a rag, everyone wipe off his shoes as best you can. Later, I'll try to give you girls a nice hair-do."

It felt good working in anticipation of an actual rescue. Everyone joined in. The boys even tried to shine the metal buttons on their trousers. By nightfall the children were as neat and tidy as was possible under the circumstances.

As the shadows deepened, Neal and John again took their places under the shrubs by the edge of the road. A black-billed coo-coo nesting nearby protested their presence with a call that sounded like a rusty hinge while the rhythmic throbbing of the katydids in the trees overhead drowned out many lesser nighttime noises. Neal edged as close to the road as possible, turned on his side and placed his ear close to the ground.

"What are you doing? Does you ear hurt?" asked John.

"No, silly, I'm listening for the sound of hoof beats. Miss Mandy said sometimes sound travels through the ground before we hear it in the air." He stayed in that position until his hip began hurting then sat up. "I guess it's easier listening this way. Do you see anything?"

"No, not yet. I wish they'd hurry up and come. The mosquitoes are eating me alive. Wait! I think I see something! Yes! A horse is coming! I think I hear a wagon, too."

Neal strained to look through the thick darkness. A shadowy form of horse and wagon slowly emerged from the darkness.

Throwing caution to the wind, John crawled out from beneath the bushes and shouted, "Here we are! Over here!"

"Shhhh!" whispered Neal, grabbing at John's pant leg to drag him back under cover. "Do you want the soldiers to hear you?" But John, in his excitement, just shouted louder.

"Miss Mandy! We're saved! The wagon's here! Hurry!" Not knowing whether to run back to the shed or go to the wagon, he elected to jump up and down beside the road. Neal looked at him in disgust then ran to where the wagon was waiting.

"Are you Smith LaFarge from Pendleton?" he asked the tallest outline on the seat.

"The very same," replied a deep voice. "Go hurry everyone along. It's best not to tarry on these roads at night. Toby, here, will help you with your baggage."

Neal turned toward the shed but the ruckus John had made had alerted everyone and they came tumbling from out their hiding place.

"Smith! It's so good of you to come!" exclaimed Mandy. "I can hardly believe you're here. Girls, hurry now. Up into the wagon. Where's Alex? Move over, Susan. Lizzie, you sit on Neal's lap." Almost hysterical with relief, Mandy babbled on, releasing the pent-up stress of her long, dangerous journey.

As soon as the last child was in place, and the valises tucked into corners, Smith turned the horse and set it smartly trotting toward home. There were a million questions Mandy wanted to ask but Smith had warned them to keep their conversation to a minimum. After several hours of jouncing, Mandy felt the wagon slow and turn. She craned her neck looking for familiar landmarks but could see only shadowy silhouettes. Suddenly the outline of a large house loomed into view and the scent of roses in bloom filled her nostrils. Here and there a flickering candle flame was seen through a darkened window and in the distance several dogs barked. As the wagon came to a halt, Toby jumped down, grasped her arm and helped her descend. In seconds all the children were unloaded and shepherded into the large front hallway of the plantation house where curious children and adults awaited them.

"Welcome to Meadow Wood," said a gentle voice. "I'm Lynette LaFarge. We are so happy you have arrived safely. Do sit down while Hannah prepares tea. There is buttermilk and corn bread for the children in the kitchen. We've a bathing tub ready for you after you've eaten. Can I get you anything else?" The candle's glow revealed a short woman with chiseled features and dark hair twisted into a chignon who was obviously expecting a child. Her excellent posture and air of authority bespoke mistress of the house. Around her clustered several children of various ages. In Mandy's state of exhaustion everything seemed fuzzy. She opened her mouth to express her gratitude but nothing came out. It was Katie who came to her rescue.

"We are so grateful to you for helping us," she said with a sweet smile. "I think we are all a bit overwhelmed by the fact we are finally in Pendleton. The walking seemed endless, sometimes. Miss Mandy bore the brunt of the adventure and is worn to a frazzle. I fear none of us are at our best."

"You poor dears!" piped a reedy, soprano voice as a matronly woman reeking of perfume waddled over to embrace Susan and Lizzie who were standing beside Mandy with bewildered looks on their faces. "You girls come with Miss Maude. She'll make everything right. Do you like corn bread and honey? Let's go sink our teeth into some right now." Cooing and cuddling, she herded the youngsters toward the kitchen with promises of an endless supply of food while Neal, Katie and Beth remained at Mandy's side.

A few minutes later, the maid, Hannah, arrived carrying a tea tray filled with sliced apple cake, dark bread, jam, tea and buttermilk. Carefully she placed it on the circular walnut table in the parlor where a single lighted lamp cast a weak, yellow glow.

"Help yourself. Please don't stand on ceremony," urged Mrs. LaFarge. "I do not expect social conversation after all you've been through. We are happy you are well and safe. Don't worry about the children. Miss Maude is my mother and will tend them as her own. When you have finished, call Hannah. She will help you with your baths. Please excuse me. I must return to bed. The doctor wants me to get as much rest as possible." She gave them a gentle smile and departed.

The minute she disappeared from sight, Katie, Beth and Neal made a beeline for the food. With trembling hand, Mandy poured herself a cup of tea, inhaling the sweet scent of a beverage long denied. Tea! Real English tea! Never would she have imagined how luxurious a cup of imported tea would seem. She took a deep draught, feeling the hot liquid flow gently through her system, then gulped the remainder as if afraid it would disappear from her cup.

"Have some apple cake, Miss Mandy. It's delicious. Here, let me fill your cup for you." Katie hovered over her mistress as if she were a child. Mandy responded numbly, feeling as weak and helpless as a newborn kitten. She gazed at her surroundings: the rich damask drapes, walnut furniture, glowing silver pieces and thick oriental rugs. We've come to the right place. There is no lack here, she thought. After several cups of tea and a generous helping of cake she felt somewhat relieved.

"Please look after the others," she said to the trio beside her after they had eaten their fill. "Help them bathe and put them to bed, then tend to yourselves. I'll give our dirty clothes to one of the servants to wash. Don't worry about me. I'll be along in a little while." Left alone, Mandy fingered her little silver cross and uttered a brief prayer of thanksgiving for a safe journey. Scarcely had she begun to relax when Smith, after cooling down his horse, entered the room. He looked at her tenderly.

"From barefoot lass to beautiful matron. I confess I feared the worst when I got your letter. I really did not expect you to come all this way without serious problems but Miss Maude reports that all the children seem to be in the best of health. I'm sorry we have not been in touch since my marriage. Taking on a ready-made family and overseeing two large farms has taken all my attention. I'm looking forward to catching up on the past five years. I'm sure you and Lynette will enjoy each other's company. Your being here is no imposition. Lynette is a gracious woman and will gladly do all she can to make you comfortable. We are in the process of redoing the second floor of the carriage house for you but it will be another week before it's ready. My mother-in-law had been living there but lately the steep steps have taken their toll so she has moved into a large room at the back of the house."

"Oh, dear! I hope we are not causing problems, Smith. I just didn't know where else to turn for protection and God did seem to indicate we were to come to Pendleton. You always seemed so wise and organized I just naturally assumed you would be my knight in shining armor and rescue us." Mandy, still holding her cross, twisted it nervously.

"As soon as I can I will look for a place of my own. I have a small inheritance but unfortunately most of my money is in confederate currency that is almost worthless now. While we are here, please let us help in any way we can. The boys are sturdy. Farm work will be good for them. Katie and Beth are skilled in sewing and cooking. I will do anything to help out; you know that." Mandy's forehead wrinkled with the effort of pleading her case.

"I know you, Miss Mandy. By week's end all the children on the plantation, including mine, will be marching to the beat of your drum. I have never met such an energetic woman. I already have plans for you: the children need a schoolteacher. The local schoolmaster left for the army six months ago leaving the task of educating the town's children to each individual family. Some children, including my own, have not fared well. Lynette is in a delicate condition; birthing babies is not easy for her. If you will hold classes from nine in the morning until one o'clock when the children are usually dismissed for dinner, it would help us all.

"The spring planting is completed and most of the farms still have a few loyal people remaining so I think we can get through the summer profitably. There's no telling when this war will end as neither side seems to be winning a majority of the skirmishes. So far, we are just systematically eliminating a whole generation of valiant, young men. A terrible travesty." Smith shook his head sorrowfully.

"Well, I've burdened you enough for one night," he said, ruefully. "Rest is what you need now. Please stay in bed as long as you wish tomorrow. We won't stand on ceremony until next week. Let the children get acquainted and explore their surroundings for a few days. Remember, there are Union scouts patrolling the area and occasionally a regiment is seen passing by, so it is best if they stay within earshot of the house.

"Lynette is already gathering clothes for your brood and I

will arrange to have some material brought in so you can sew dresses suitable for your role as schoolmistress. Whatever you need, just ask for. Where there's a will, there's a way." After tamping out his pipe and tossing the ashes into the fireplace, Smith strode out of the room.

Mandy listened to his receding steps. How secure he made her feel. Perhaps she should begin to search for a husband. It would be wonderful to have a shoulder to lean on and a heart willing to share her hopes and dreams. She roused herself from her wishful thinking and walked slowly to the kitchen for a long awaited bath.

It was two o'clock the next afternoon before Mandy woke and even then she did not feel like getting up. The soft cotton sheets caressed her skin while the fresh, flower-laden air made her breathe so deeply she seemed to be in a trance-like state. She tossed and turned for a while hoping to continue her rest, but when sleep evaded her she began to feel guilty at being abed in the middle of the afternoon. Swinging her legs to the floor, she immediately noticed a lovely blue calico day dress complete with petticoats and a silk chemise draped over a near-by chair. Fine cotton stockings lay folded on top of supple leather slippers. With a soft cry of delight she drew the silk underwear over her body. How wonderful it felt! She dressed slowly, reveling in the softness of the fabrics. Finally, she used the silver-backed comb and brush set on the dresser to arrange her hair. Feeling like a new woman, she went down the steep rear stairs to the kitchen.

"Miss Mandy's awake!" Lizzie announced to the others who were in the hallway playing games. Suddenly the kitchen was filled with eager voices relating the wonders of the farm and new friends.

"Please, one at a time!" Mandy laughed, holding up her

hands to stop the flow of strident voices. "Let me have a cup of tea to sip while I listen." She found a kettle of water simmering on the woodstove and filled a teapot with loose tea leaves. Soon the amber brew filled her cup. "Ah, that's much better. Now, Lizzie and Susan first."

"We found some baby kittens and Molly showed us a nest with hawks in it. Sam got stung by a bee but Katie put mud on the bump. There are chickens here and pigs, too. We got to pet a baby pig. It felt prickly." Lizzie rattled on until she ran out of breath.

Both girls' eyes were as round as saucers as they related their adventures. Mandy listened, amazed at how resilient their young bodies were. Less than a day after their long journey, the children seemingly were back to normal.

John told of the vast expanse of farmland and of the livestock scattered in various hidden meadows. Sam remarked about the different varieties of bugs found in the area. He had already started a collection in a bush by the carriage house. Katie and Beth rapturously described the beautiful flowerbeds and gardens surrounding the house. They presented themselves to Mandy in new cotton dresses, whirling around to show their pleasure in the newfound finery.

"Where are Neal and Alex?" Mandy asked, buttering a leftover biscuit.

"They went with Mr. LaFarge to inspect a field of cotton. They'll be back by suppertime," stated John. "My leg feels fine. There is just a small scab left. Can I go with them next time?"

Mandy smiled. As she had hoped, the farm activities had absorbed them all.

The euphoric climate lasted four days, then Mandy noticed sides were being drawn: the LaFarge children against her family. At first there was just the occasional outburst of accusations which the adults tried to ignore in the hope that the problems would work themselves out. Later, it escalated to the point that if one child entered the room another would abruptly leave. The tension at the dinner table gave most of the adults a slight case of indigestion and was upsetting to all.

"What's going on?" Mandy asked Katie that evening as she helped her bathe Susan and Lizzie.

"The LaFarge children are jealous of us. They say we are eating too much of their food and causing too much work for the servants."

"I see," said Mandy, thoughtfully. "Have you tried being especially kind, including them in your games?"

"Yes, but they always have an excuse why they don't want to play with us so now we just ignore them." Katie scrubbed Lizzie's back vigorously, causing her to yelp.

"Hmmm," Mandy murmured as she rinsed Susan's hair.

The next morning she called a family meeting in her room. "The strife between you and the LaFarge children has gone on long enough. I want to remind you we are guests here. Without the kindness of the LaFarge family we would probably be living in an abandoned shed somewhere, doing without food or other creature comforts. There are only three days left before school starts so do your best to mend whatever fences you need to so harmony will prevail again. It is not healthy for Mrs. LaFarge to deal with excessive stress in her condition.

"Now, here are your duties for the rest of the week: Katie and Beth are to sew nightgowns and underwear for Susan and Lizzie; Neal and John are to help Mr. LaFarge wherever he needs them; Sam and Alex will run errands for me and keep the wood box filled; and Susan and Lizzie must keep our rooms tidy. As soon as I am assured an income from teaching, I will look for a house of our own to rent. Living here is only temporary so let's leave a good impression." Mandy smiled lovingly at them. "You are wonderful people and I love you very much. I know you will do your best. Shoo, now. You may play until noon."

Everyone scattered like leaves in a brisk wind. Mandy walked to the window facing the vegetable garden. She would divide her day by working outside in the morning and sewing in the afternoon. It was important each child have respectable clothes for church. She wondered whether she should attend the Old Stone Church frequented by the Low Country aristocrats or go to the church in town where the sharecroppers and local people went. When she had lived in Pendleton years ago, she had gone to both depending on their programs. She decided to ask Smith what he preferred her to do. They had not conversed privately since the night of her arrival. During the day he oversaw the remaining field hands, after dinner he worked on his accounts or repaired broken machinery. In the evening he retired with his family to a private area of the house. Although she longed to discuss her decisions with him, she did not want to impose or create any improper suppositions.

"I must find a place of my own as soon as possible," said Mandy to a stray cat that had jumped onto the window seat to enjoy a patch of sun. First, she needed to find a trustworthy banker who could arrange to have her monthly inheritance deposited locally. These days money was not that necessary as there was little to buy. Everyone had learned to become self-sufficient since the Yankee soldiers occasionally pillaged the area. Each family grew what they food they could and made do with whatever clothes they had.

The situation in Pendleton really was no different than in Charleston except here there were no military exercises going on or unruly soldiers prowling the streets. The days of imported delicacies were gone, at least until after the war. She noticed the household menu rarely changed. Perhaps her family was eating too much. How much was too much when it came to feeding growing children? Well, she could do some of the cooking. She enjoyed creating new recipes from whatever wild game and vegetables were available. She decided to look for an opportunity to tactfully volunteer her services.

"Miss Mandy! Come quick! Sam stepped on a bee's nest and they stung him all over! Hurry!" Alex burst into the room in a panic. Mandy ran to the back porch where Sam was crying hysterically, his face and arms covered with red welts.

"Katie! Boil some water quickly! I'll get parsley from the herb garden." Mandy snatched several handfuls of the emerald green plant, soaked them in the boiling water, then applied rags dipped in the parsley juice to the bee stings. She could see Sam's left eye swelling shut and there were even bumps in his hair. Before long he was covered with medicated cloths, making him look like an Egyptian mummy. In his distress, he sought privacy in the rose garden and curled up in a grapevine chair.

Little Rose Ellen, the youngest LaFarge child, followed closely behind and solemnly stared at him until he began to squirm in embarrassment. "Would you like to hold my dolly?" she asked, offering him a battered rag doll with cornhusk curls. "It will make you feel better. She's such a comfort."

"No, thank you," he replied. "I'm afraid the wet rags may stain her. But I would like a drink of water." He pointed to the pump several yards away.

Rose Ellen stood up, carefully laying her doll against the chair back. With a determined look on her face she toddled to the well pump, stretched as far upward as she could, grasp the pump handle and began the tedious task of forcing water out of the spout and into the bucket beneath the pump. Soon her little face was red with the effort and her breath came in short gasps. As a tiny stream of water began to trickle into the bucket she gauged the amount needed to fill a cup then stopped pumping. Scooping up the water, she presented it to Sam as if it were the elixir of life.

Sam drank greedily. "That was good, Rose Ellen. Thank you. You are stronger than I thought."

The little girl smiled broadly. "You are my own dear Sam," she replied, patting his rag-covered hand. Then, cuddling her doll, she trudged toward the house.

It's too bad the other LaFarge children aren't as sweet as she is, thought Sam. She is the only one unaware of the war's influence on the farm. To the others we are just more mouths to feed. Suddenly he understood the reason the children had distanced themselves. They were afraid of losing what little they had. He resolved to help in every way he could as soon as he was able. In the meantime he would share his insight with Katie and Neal. Perhaps they could come up with a solution.

Later that afternoon, Mandy decided to familiarize herself with the school and its surroundings. After a mile walk, she stood outside the small, wooden building and analyzed its physical properties. It seemed unusually austere compared to the large brick schools in Charleston with their landscaped yards. Then she remembered this building was mainly for the local residents of Pendleton. In normal times the summer families returned to their homes in the low country in November after there had been a hard frost to kill the mosquitoes. However, because of the war, most of the families opted for the peace and security of Pendleton, especially since so many of the rice plantations had been burned or taken over by the Union officers.

Taking a deep breath, she climbed the two wooden steps, turned the brass doorknob and stepped inside. The long windows on each side let in enough light to encourage reading; the pine floor was swept clean and the room looked neat and inviting. She counted thirty desks and several extra benches as she walked to the front to examine the teacher's large, oak desk that looked sturdy and formidable. She pulled open one of the four side drawers and discovered a box full of chalk for both herself and her students. Another drawer was filled with essay size paper and several bottles of ink. The former teacher must have made a supreme effort to keep the children supplied with the basics for learning, she thought.

Mandy sat in the matching oak straight back chair, leaned her arms on the desk and surveyed her surrounding. Teaching thirty children of varying ages would be a daunting task and one totally out of her area of expertise. How would she keep order? A nervous shiver ran down her spine. She closed her eyes and tried to remember her days in Mrs. Robeleau's finishing school. She had been one of sixteen girls, all fourteen or older, most of whom were being instructed in the same lesson at the same time. Mrs. Robeleau ruled with an iron fist, a loud voice and weekly reports to parents. Mandy did not think she could function like that. She wasn't inclined toward corporate punishment. Her goal was to encourage the love of learning by example instead of force. Well, Monday would reveal all. Perhaps what she lacked in experience she could counter with enthusiasm.

"Lord Jesus, help me. Guide me and give me patience, wisdom and tolerance. Please let the children like me. I know I can do all things if You help me." She buried her face in her hands for a few moments then rose, resolutely walked down the aisle and out into the summer heat, closing the door firmly behind her.

"Everybody on the porch for a meeting," Mandy ordered after breakfast the next morning. "Katie, go find the boys, Sam and John got away before I could corral them. Beth, help me finish dressing Lizzie and Susan." She quickly ran a brush through Susan's blond curls then tied them back away from her face.

"Put your sandals on, Lizzie," Beth said, tossing the little girl her shoes. "No, not that foot. Good, you're learning. Go get your dolly to play with."

Mandy arranged everyone in a semi-circle around her. A cool breeze kept the gnats away and helped her retain her composure. "As you all know, school starts Monday. Because I have been asked to fill in for the schoolmaster until he returns, our mornings will be a bit hectic until we have worked out a schedule. Here are some suggestions." Mandy emphasized the word to stress its importance. "Katie and Beth will dress and look after Lizzie and Susan. Miss Maude has graciously volunteered to watch them along with the LaFarge youngsters but I don't want to add to her burden so make sure they have eaten their fill, are properly dressed and know where their dolls are. Neal and John are responsible for Alex and Sam. That means making sure they have their school supplies, are properly dressed, and so forth. You must also look after them at school in case of bullying or teasing. We are newcomers so I expect some pranks will be played, just don't let them get out of hand. Make sure the other children understand that we stick together as a family. However, during school hours you are just regular students, I will not play favorites or show partiality. I will have to leave the house before you in the morning in order to arrive at school before the first student does. For the first few weeks I will probably be preoccupied with my teaching responsibilities so I apologize in advance for neglecting you all a bit. Do you think you can manage all that?"

"Don't worry. We can handle ourselves. Nobody will bother us. We're tougher than most of the children around here," Neal replied with an air of bravado.

"When am I going to have time to get dressed and fix my hair?" complained Beth. "Susan and Lizzie always dawdle so at breakfast."

"You and Katie will have to work out the details. If the girls haven't finished eating by the time you must leave, they will have to go hungry until dinnertime. They'll learn soon enough to eat faster.

"Soon the carriage house rooms will be completed and we will have a temporary place of our own. It will mean even more work for all of you because we will not have any servants, but at least it will seem more like our past life in Charleston. I promise you as soon as I am able I will rent a house. For now though, we must be thankful for the generosity of friends. Any suggestions? No? All right, when your chores are finished, you are free to go play. Please be nice to the LaFarge children."

Like a herd of stampeding elephants, everyone bounded off in all directions, anxious to put the words 'work and responsibility' as far from them as possible. Mandy went to her room to remake her one good dress into a suitable teacher's attire.

Despite her instructions, Monday morning was bedlam. Tempers flared, faces scowled and uncustomary shouts of defiance echoed through the rooms. Mandy ignored the many opportunities to referee her family and hurried to school well before the first child arrived. The July heat was oppressive even in the early morning. She hoped the windows opened or classes would have to be held outside in the shade. By eight-thirty twelve students had arrived and Mandy could see her charges marching in various stages of disarray up the front steps.

"Good morning, boys and girls. Please take a seat wherever you like, for now," she hastily added. "My name is Miss Greene. I will be your teacher for the time being. As I point to you, please come up to my desk and tell me your name and grade so I may be able to group you properly."

By the time Mandy had registered the first arrivals, ten more children had appeared. By mid-morning only two desks were vacant and Mandy was beside herself trying to cope with assignments.

"Really, Miss Greene, you don't seem experienced enough to teach us older students," stated one teen girl in an affected tone. "I told my mother the Pendleton school would be too elementary. I've already had two years of French. Parlez-vous bien Francais?"

"Oui. Et si vous croyez que vous etes trop avancee pour ce cours, vous pouvez disposer." Mandy retorted, two bright red spots of anger appearing on her cheeks.

The girl blushed in embarrassment and busily began to rearrange her books.

"Take that, Miss High and Mighty," Mandy said under her breath while forcing a bright smile. Her struggles with the French language had proven worthwhile after all. "Class,

I've come to the conclusion that will be fair to all, I think. I realize you normally do not attend school in this oppressive summer heat. Therefore, a full day's instruction will be extremely taxing on all of us physically and mentally. I propose we divide the day in half. I will teach grades one through four in the morning from eight o'clock to eleven. Grades five and up will convene at eleven fifteen and dismiss at two. I'm sorry that you older children may have to change your dinner hour but there is not that much to eat right now, anyway.

"The early grades will be taught in the usual way but the afternoon class will concentrate on only two topics at a time so we may study them in depth. We will start with literature and geography. To take advantage of any wandering breezes the afternoon class will meet under the oaks in the side yard. Bring something to sit on and wear cool clothing. We will save our fine attire for a special function.

"Here is the assignment for the afternoon class: write a two hundred word essay on an event that impacted your life or on your future aspirations including your goals for reaching them. Come get paper and ink. You may do your writing now, then leave when you are finished. Grades one through four come to the front so I can review your reading skills."

After a few muted grumbles, the older students settled down to writing. Mandy could hear in the background the scratch of pens on paper as she listened to younger children stumble through their readers. The previous teacher was to be commended, she thought. Even the youngest child knew his letters and could read simple words.

By noon the heat in the schoolhouse was stifling. Mandy's hands were so sticky with sweat she blurred the ink on the essays as she held them. Perspiration glistened on the faces of the children as they made frequent trips to the water bucket.

"Children, that is enough for today. You've all done very well. Please try to be on time tomorrow so we can begin promptly at eight. Class dismissed."

Sighs of relief from all corners of the room assured Mandy she had made the right decision. She remained at her desk until the last child had left the pathway then gathered her paraphernalia and trudged home, exhausted.

"I never realized how stressful teaching is," remarked Mandy to Lynette during dinner. "As a whole the children were well behaved and attentive but keeping track of the minds of twenty-eight students takes great effort. I don't know how the former schoolmaster did it."

"I know he was a strict disciplinarian and often used the older children as helpers," replied Lynette. "A practice I fervently deplore. The older students need to be challenged scholastically just as much as the beginners. I'm not sure he realized that." She salted a portion of summer squash then sprinkled it with parsley.

"I declare I'm even beginning to like this horrid, old yellow squash. When times were good I never ate anything so bland and common. Now I'll eat anything that doesn't look as if it wants to eat me first."

Mandy smiled. Her youthful days on the Tennessee farm had taught her to appreciate simple foods. Her mother would stew a squirrel or rabbit with whatever vegetables were available then drop pastry made from flour and water into the boiling broth after everything else had cooked. Dumpling stew had been on the menu several times a week back then.

"Miss Mandy, we played with kittens and helped Miss Maude wind balls of yarn." Susan's voice cut through Mandy's reverie. The little girl stood in the doorway, still rumpled from her late afternoon nap. "Where's Katie? I want her to brush my hair and fix my shoes so I can go out and play. Mmmmm, that looks good. Can I have some?" Susan sidled up to the table and pointed to the dish of squash.

Mandy put a spoonful on a plate, sprinkled it with parsley and salt and set it in front of Susan who sampled a slice, chewing it carefully.

"Honey would make it go down better," she concluded, sliding off her chair. "I'm going to look for Katie."

"I am amazed at how much better Susan is talking since she has other children to play with," remarked Mandy. "In retrospect I think my brood waited on her too much, meeting her needs before she even had to ask. Thankfully your children have not tried to spoil her. I'm sure school will have a soothing effect on everyone.

"If you don't mind, Lynette, I think I'll retire to the parlor where I can have some privacy for a few minutes. I've dealt with little people enough for one day. I need some solitude. Excuse me." Mandy poured herself a cup of tea then walked toward the front of the house, being careful not to be seen. Sinking into an overstuffed chair, she stared vacantly out of the window at the front lawn where several sheep and goats in separate areas grazed under the shade of the pecan trees. Soon her eye caught the flutter of gray wings as a mockingbird arrived with a green worm in its beak to feed its fledglings nesting in a hawthorn tree nearby.

Young minds are as hungry as baby birds, she mused. I must feed them intellectual information that is moral and godly. Regardless how inappropriate truth may seem sometimes, it must be taught. When the war ends no doubt we will be faced with some unpleasant realities. There is no time like the present to encourage people to embrace truth instead of substituting past traditions and beliefs. Change must come and with it the knowledge that all people are God's creation. Every person has the right to honest pay for an honest day's work and the freedom to pursue happiness and success. I must try to instill that concept into my students' minds, she thought. She raised her arms and stretched wearily. Today her inexperience and shortcomings seemed overwhelming. Hopefully, as the days progressed she would feel more capable in her new position.

Evenings found Mandy hard at work preparing lesson plans or reading voraciously about the subjects she was teaching. It took all her extra time to stay ahead of some of her students. Several of the older girls had traveled to Europe and looked down their noses at a teacher who had not had a 'continental' experience. Silently she blessed Mrs. Robeleau for being such a strict teacher and insisting on a well-rounded education. She may not have seen the London Bridge but she knew every incident in its history and could converse in French with the fluency of a native Parisian. She would show them just how knowledgeable a teacher she was.

Chapter Six

"Well, Miss Mandy, the carriage house rooms are finally ready for your inspection," Smith said, as the adults relaxed at the dinner table with their evening tea. "At the moment all we have in the way of paint is whitewash but I'm sure you will be able to make the place attractive and homey."

"How wonderful just to have a place of our own!" exclaimed Mandy. Then, afraid she had offended her hostess, she added, "Oh, please, I did not mean our accommodations here have not been satisfactory. You have been more than gracious. I am only happy to again relinquish your lovely rooms to your family. I realize the children have not been as cooperative as they could be. Perhaps separating them will have some advantages. I'm sure the nine of us have been overwhelming, at times. Now I will set up my own housekeeping including meals and laundry so your lives can return to normal."

"These past weeks have truly been a new experience for us, but a satisfactory one. Each child is a delight in his own special way. You are to be commended as a parent," replied Lynette. "If I were not in this condition I could better cope with all the challenges. It's times like these I really appreciate my mother's love of little ones." She smiled at Smith who reached for her hand.

"Lynette has the patience of Job," he said. "Her gentle spirit captured my heart the moment I met her. She is my inspiration and my reward." He pressed her hand to his lips while gazing lovingly into her eyes.

Mandy gave an involuntary shiver. She felt she was intruding in a very intimate moment while at the same time she yearned for someone to love her as passionately and openly as Smith did his wife. What would it be like, she wondered, to wake each morning to the companionship of one who had pledged both love and sustenance forever? She remembered Smith's arms around her when they had danced together. She had been too young to enjoy his masculinity then, but now…

"Please excuse me," she said, rising hastily. "I will have the children gather their belongings and get organized so we can move into the carriage house tomorrow morning. Thank you so much for all you have done for us. I pray God's richest blessings on you.

"I will take my tea to my room as I have some lessons to prepare." Mandy walked quickly to her room and closed the door. Setting the teacup on the dresser, she knelt beside her bed.

"O heavenly Father, I have seen true love between a man and woman tonight and it has aroused desires I did not know existed in me. Please, if it be Thy will, find a husband for me. I know it won't be easy, for who would want such a large ready-made family? Nevertheless, the Bible says nothing is impossible for You, dear Lord. Bless Smith and Lynette and their family, especially the babe that is to come. Please give Lynette an easy delivery. She seems so frail. Thank You for finding us this place. Let their sacrifice not be in vain. In Jesus' name, amen."

The very act of praying soothed Mandy's spirit. Once again in control of her emotions, she gulped her tea then went to tell her family of tomorrow's move to the carriage house.

Living in their own space worked wonders. Although they had little in the way of furnishings, just being alone together calmed everyone. Mandy drew up a list of duties for each child and saw they were carried out daily. Neal and John continued to help on the farm and supply the family with wild meat. Katie and Beth took over household responsibilities while Mandy worked on lesson plans and tutored students who were falling behind. Sam and Alex pulled weeds in Mandy's little garden, often sneaking off to fish during free time. Susan and Lizzie played house or ran through the yard after stray ducks and kittens. They were 'on call' for when little jobs arose.

On the night of August seventeenth Mandy was wakened by a servant calling, "Miss Mandy, come quickly! The baby is wantin' to be born!" Grabbing her robe, she told Katie to stay with the children and hurried into the big house. Smith met her with a worried smile.

"I've sent for the midwife. Our doctor is with the troops in Columbia this week. See what you can do to comfort Lynette. She does not want her mother present as Miss Maude gets too excited which strains her weak heart. I know you are not experienced in such matters but at least you are of the same sex. I've told the servants to gather towels and warm some water. That's about all I know to do, except worry."

"I'm sure everything will be fine. Lynette has already borne three fine children. By this time she probably knows as much about the procedure as does the doctor. I'll sit with her until the mid-wife comes." Mandy climbed the front curving staircase and quietly entered the bedroom where Lynette lay moaning softly.

"Every time I give birth I curse the day Eve ate the forbidden fruit and brought God's judgment of birth pangs on us," Lynette said through clenched teeth. "I don't understand why we have to suffer anew with each birth. Once would be enough for a lifetime." She gave a sudden gasp and pulled on the birthing rags tied to the bedposts.

"Where is the midwife? This baby is anxious to start life in this miserable world. Mandy, have Hannah boil the embroidery scissors and fetch the silk thread from my sewing basket. We'll have to manage as best we can. Get some old papers and plenty of clean rags and towels for cleaning up. Hurry!"

Mandy ran to the staircase, shouted Hannah her instructions, then dashed to the morning room where by the light of a flickering candle she searched feverishly for the silk thread and scissors. Within minutes everything was ready.

"Wash your hands, Mandy. The baby's coming. You will have to gently support him as he emerges," gasped Lynette.

Mandy did as she was told then watched with awe as a tiny head appeared followed by a shoulder and finally the rest of the body, landing safely in Mandy's outstretched hands. "It's a boy!" she exclaimed.

"Wash his face with a wet, clean rag, then tie the thread tightly in two places on the umbilical cord and cut between them," instructed Lynette in an exhausted voice.

As Mandy wiped the tiny face the baby puckered up and began to cry. Quickly she cut the cord, cleaned the baby's wrinkled body, wrapped him in a soft blanket and placed him in Lynette's arms just as the midwife came bursting through the door.

"Oh, dear," she said, surveying the scene. "It seems Mother Nature was in control this time. Well, lets have a look at you, Mrs. LaFarge. Did the afterbirth come out cleanly?" She placed her hands on Lynette's stomach and massaged it carefully.

"I didn't see anything but the baby and a bit of fine tissue around him," stated Mandy, wondering if she had done something wrong.

"The body must expel all the afterbirth, otherwise hemorrhaging or putrefaction could occur," explained the midwife.

Mandy watched the massaging with interest. She had once seen the birth of a mule and remembered the pinkish-gray sac the mare had dropped after the foal's birth. So women did somewhat the same. She shook her head in amazement.

There was a sudden rush of blood and tissue which the midwife caught in old newspaper. After that she bathed Lynette, helped her change into a fresh nightgown, and plumped the pillows. "Is this your first birthin'?" she asked Mandy. "You did a fine job with the baby. Now you know more'n you did yesterday. Life's excitin', ain't it, Miss?"

Mandy nodded. Where would she be when her first baby arrived on the scene? Who would be its father? Would she have competent help when she needed it? For a moment her mind was filled with anxious thoughts but soon a gentle peace descended. She had given her life to Jesus Christ. Her future as well as the present was in His hands.

At the midwife's permission, Smith entered the room. "My dearest Lynette, my darling. You have given me a fine son.

Praise God all is well." He hovered over his wife and baby, tears of joy streaming down his face.

Mandy quietly slipped from the room to allow them the privacy they deserved. To her surprise the sky was streaked with dawn light. Where had the time gone? A feeling of exhaustion made her cling momentarily to the carriage house stair railing. Thankfully, today was Saturday so she had no teaching obligations. After reporting to Katie that all was well and a beautiful baby boy had been added to the LaFarge family, she snuggled deeply into the sheets and slept.

The smell of rabbit stew awoke her hours later. Dressing in haste she joined her family just as they were about to sit down to dinner. "Thank you for letting me sleep in," she said. "My, what a fine meal you've prepared. I could go away for a month and you'd never even miss me. I'm so proud of your independence. I don't have to worry about you, I know things will turn out right in the end."

Later in the day, Rose Ellen came over to announce the baby's birth. "We've got a new brother. He's got red hair and blue eyes. His face is wrinkly but mama says the wrinkles will go away soon. Daddy named him after Grandpa Du Bois but we can give him a nickname."

"That's nice, Rose Ellen," Mandy murmured. "Why don't you play with Susan for a while? She is under the oak tree by the back porch." After making sure everyone was well occupied, Mandy escaped down the woods path for some quiet time. She spied a large tree with a low branch suitable for sitting. Giggling like a schoolgirl, she grabbed the branch with both hands and swung herself up into its crouch. Boldly she climbed as high as she could until she could see the mountains, like ancient sentinels, on the horizon. She had always drawn strength from their unchanging mass.

Mandy's Carriage House Saga

"I will lift mine eyes unto the hills. From whence cometh my strength? My strength cometh from the Lord of hosts," she quoted from Psalm 121. A red fox trotted beneath her tree. Mandy watched as he sniffed for a scent that might provide his dinner. A blue jay screamed a warning, causing an eerie silence to fall over the woods. When the fox went on his way, a chipmunk sounded the all clear and the hustle and bustle of woodland life began anew.

What a wonderful lesson, Mandy thought. When danger is present, be still and invisible. Let it pass by unchallenged. Then pick up the pattern of life again. She wondered if that was what the Pendleton residents were doing about the war; letting it pass by while living quiet lives. Some women were frantic to hear from a son or husband but they said little about it. The phrase 'no news is good news' did not sit lightly on their bowed shoulders. 'Any news is preferred over no news' would more aptly describe their lot. All at once she was glad she did not have a sweetheart to worry about. God in His wisdom knew she could not concentrate on raising eight orphans and worry about a soul mate at the same time. She smiled at the new revelation about herself. There was a season for everything; learning to be patient and trust God's timing was the challenge. With agile grace she swung down from her perch and walked contentedly homeward.

By Monday morning most of Pendleton had heard the good news of the LaFarge baby boy. With so many boys and men dying in the war, a male baby was regarded as a special gift from God for replenishing the Southern heritage. A baby shower was planned for after Lynette had regained her strength. Folks felt it was important during these times to socialize as much as possible to keep a close community spirit.

Thursday Neal rode out to inspect the cattle Smith had hidden in an obscure pasture at the far end of his property. As he trotted along the edge of the woods, a glint of metal caught his attention. Quickly he dismounted and hid behind a thick alder bush. After waiting for what seemed like an hour for a patrol or scout to pass by, he crept closer to where he had seen the reflection. A strange patch of blue was mingled with the pasture grass. Holding his breath in fear, he advanced, weaving from tree to tree for protection. When he was about ten feet from the blue patch he carefully stood up for a better view. There before him lay the body of a Yankee soldier. Was he dead or injured? Neal coughed gently to announce his presence but there was no movement so he edged nearer.

"Hey, mister. Are you alive?" he asked. He was close enough now to see the rusty stain of blood from a bullet wound on the upper back of the soldier's jacket. After finding a stout stick to use as a weapon, he carefully walked to where the soldier lay face down in the grass. With obvious distaste, Neal reached for a hand to feel for a pulse. The skin was cold and clammy but there was a slight pulse indicating the man was still alive. He stood over the body, uncertain what to do. The man was an enemy soldier but at the same time he was a human being. Wasn't one of the Ten Commandments an edict not to kill? If he left the man to die would God consider him a murderer? Perhaps the soldier had a family who would mourn his death as keenly as Neal had mourned the death of his own father and mother.

"I'll be right back," he whispered to the still body as he mounted his horse and urged it into a gallop. Riding along he formed a plan: he would not tell anyone about the soldier except Miss Mandy who was sure to want to help. His mission would be nursing the soldier back to health while probing for Union army secrets. Perhaps he could learn some Union strategies which he could report to Confederate headquarters. He rode directly to the schoolhouse where he met Mandy as she was leaving for the day.

"Miss Mandy! Come with me! I've something to show you. It's a secret but I need your help."

"Slow down, Neal. I can't understand you. What's the matter? Look at Windy; you've ridden him too hard. He's all sweaty. Get down and walk that poor animal while you tell me your secret."

Neal slid from Windy's back and matched his step to Mandy's. "I found a wounded soldier out by the far pasture when I went to check the cows. He's a Yankee and hurt bad. Is it alright to help him even though he's the enemy?" Neal's face contorted with anxiety and confusion. "Don't tell anyone. It's my secret."

"The Bible says do unto others as you would have them do unto you. God loves us all regardless of our political beliefs. It's our duty to help whomever we can. Let me get a few supplies then we'll tend to your soldier."

"Please don't tell Mr. LaFarge. He may not want us to help the enemy."

"Perhaps you are right, Neal. Let's see how badly the soldier is hurt and if he will need more medical help than what we can give him. Go saddle Misty for me while I get my things. Tell anyone you meet that I feel like riding today and you are accompanying me. Hurry."

Soon they were standing at the edge of the woods tying their mounts to the trees. Neal approached the soldier cautiously. "I covered him up a little with weeds so no one would see him," he said, brushing the debris from the soldier's coat.

Mandy carried her valise to where Neal was kneeling. "Oh, dear. He is in a bad way. Help me take off his jacket. I'll cut it around his arms and then we can remove the back first.

Neal, start a small fire to heat water." Mandy struggled to cut through the heavy wool of the Union uniform, eventually removing part of his coat and shirt. She could see where a bullet had come through his shoulder. The area had bled freely as evidenced by a large amount of blood on his clothing.

"I don't see any infection, thank God." She dipped small squares of muslin in the simmering water, covered them with a salve of medicinal herbs, and pressed them into the gaping hole. "We must roll him over so I can clean the other side of the wound. He needs to drink some water, too. He has lost a lot of blood."

After spreading an old sheet on the ground, they carefully turned the soldier onto his back. The motion caused him to moan and raise a leg as if to get up.

"Lie still," hissed Mandy. "You don't want the bleeding to start again. We're friends, come to help. Don't move." After cutting away the front part of the blood caked jacket and shirt Mandy studied the area where the bullet had entered. The skin around the hole was red, but there did not seem to be any pus draining from the wound. God is surely with him, thought Mandy as she cleaned the wound and packed it with ointment. After covering the wound with a clean cloth she wrapped several long strips of sheeting around his shoulder, front and back, to hold everything together.

Meanwhile, Neal washed the man's face with warm water and dribbled droplets of water into his mouth. After a few minutes there was a flicker of eyelids and Mandy found herself looking into a pair of brilliant blue eyes. She rocked back on her haunches in surprise. This was the soldier she had encountered in the woods on her way to Pendleton. She would recognize those blue eyes anywhere. A rush of compassion filled her heart. How glad she was she had agreed to help him.

"Drink as much water as you can," she encouraged. "Fortunately your wound is not infected but you have lost a goodly amount of blood. You must not move until you heal a little. This is a safe, solitary place where you can hide until you recover. My name is Miss Greene; this is Neal, who found you. You can thank God Neal has a kind heart or you may have been left to die."

"Thanks, good buddy," the soldier whispered, looking at Neal. "Lieutenant Richard Roberts at your service." Then his eyes closed as he drifted into a semi-unconscious state.

Mandy showed Neal how to build a rough lean-to of pine boughs at the edge of the woods to keep out the hot sun and rain. Together they lifted the sheet on which the soldier lay and half dragged, half carried him to the shelter.

While Mandy fussed over the soldier, wrapping him as best she could in the sheet to protect him from the deer flies and other insects that were a constant source of irritation to human and beast alike, Neal wandered through the meadow and nearby woods. He knew that a well-trained army horse would not leave his master. After a brief search, he spotted a large bay gelding grazing on a honeysuckle vine.

"Whoa, big fella," he crooned softly as he slowly approached the mount. Carefully he reached for the trailing reins, keeping his eyes on the horse in case it should rear or kick. "Gotcha, now let's go back to your master." He gave a slight tug on the reins and the horse followed him obediently.

"Miss Mandy, I caught the soldier's horse. What should we do with him? We can't take him back with us. Mr. LaFarge would want to know where we found him."

"Could you put him in the pasture with the cows?" Mandy asked. "How often does Smith check on these animals?"

"Not much right now. He has turned them over to me, so

I guess it would be all right to let the horse graze with them. I'll unsaddle him first." Neal removed the saddle which had a canteen and a leather saddlebag tied to it. Perhaps the army's secrets are in that bag, he thought. Next time I come, I'll look through it.

"Put his saddle in the shelter, Neal, so he knows his horse has been found. That will be a great comfort to him, I'm sure. You are a very competent young man to think of looking for his horse. I'm sure he will be very appreciative." Mandy smiled approvingly. "I think we've done all we can for right now, we'd best be leaving before Katie begins to worry and sends someone looking for us."

The next few days were a study in subterfuge. On the pretense of repairing the back pasture fencing, Neal returned to feed and check on Lt. Roberts each morning. On the second day to his dismay, the soldier was awake and propped up against his saddle. So much for secretly reading the contents of the saddlebag, he thought, untying a sack that bulged with fruit, biscuits, jams, books and pen and paper to help the soldier pass the time.

"Good morning, Lt. Roberts," Neal said. "How are you feeling? I brought you some food and stuff. Your horse is in the pasture just over the hill with our cows. We didn't tell anyone you are here so don't worry about being captured." He handed the soldier the sack, then stood hesitantly to one side, staring at him.

"I must let my commanding officer know I am all right," Lt. Roberts said, his eyes flashing with concern. "I usually check in every Friday after I've scouted the foothills area to make sure no new munitions works are started here. I am responsible for the lives of several platoons. As soon as I am able to walk and mount my horse, I must be on my way. What do you hear of the war?"

"I'm afraid I have no news of any kind. Smith LaFarge, the owner of the farm where we are staying, is preoccupied with his newborn son and his crops. If there were anything out of the ordinary going on I would probably hear of it. Is there to be a raid on our town?" Neal asked anxiously, his heart racing with anticipation.

"No, no. Don't fret yourself. The fighting is all to the east and south right now. I just wish I knew what was happening. I have friends in the cavalry and I fear for them."

"Oh. We are worried about our friends, too." Neal shooed the flies away with a wave of his hand. "I found you. Your rifle and your blue jacket gave you away."

"I should have known better than to wear my uniform. I had just come from an important meeting and was in a hurry to get to my next post so I left without removing my coat. It was very stupid of me. No doubt some Confederate out hunting saw me and decided to eliminate an enemy. I don't blame him. I probably would have done the same." He fell silent, chewing on a biscuit.

"Thanks for catching my horse. I'd be obliged if you kept me a secret. I am not a killer and I promise not to harm anyone. I am a scout and a runner between army camps, nothing more. Do you understand?" Lt. Roberts gave Neal a wan smile.

Neal nodded. The soldier was just another person who could have been born in the South if circumstances had been different. "Miss Mandy will come after school to change the bandage," he said. "She won't tell anyone about you either. She is very nice. I've got to go now. I'll be back tomorrow." He swung into the saddle and trotted away.

All of a sudden being a spy had lost its appeal.

It was a hot, sticky, breathless Mandy that arrived in late

afternoon to check on Lt. Roberts. Rather than go home and saddle Misty, which would have incurred the curiosity of her family because she detested horseback riding and rode only out of necessity, she opted to go directly to the meadow from the school, a distance of about a mile. As she approached the lean-to she called out softly to make the soldier aware of her presence. She was not in the mood to get shot. He raised his eyes from the book he was reading and nodded a greeting.

"I am so glad to see you sitting up," Mandy said, opening her valise and arranging her medical supplies on a towel. Gently she unwound the cloth binding and examined the wound. "Much improved," she stated, slathering ointment on each opening and applying fresh bandages. She sat back on her heels and smiled at him.

"I want to thank you for the gift of those squirrels you gave me when the children and I were on our way to Pendleton. I never did thank you properly. Those and the honey I found were the only nourishment we had that day. They were a Godsend."

"I was glad to do it. I had been trailing you for about two miles waiting for an opening to help without betraying myself. You going off by yourself was the perfect opportunity," the soldier replied. "I was amazed to see you gather honey straight from the tree without a smoking torch. That is an old Indian trick. Where did you learn it?"

"Long ago I ran away from some rather difficult circumstances. While I was on my way to Pendleton, a Cherokee Indian by the name of Soaring Hawk, came to my rescue after I had fallen down a mountain. He taught me many survival tricks. They have come in handy in various ways," smiled Mandy, thinking back on the lessons her dear friend had shown her.

"Where have you come from and where are you going?" It was time to change the subject before she became maudlin. Besides, in the interest of the security of the area, she needed to know what the Union army had in store for Pendleton. If Neal hadn't been able to wheedle information out of him, perhaps she could.

"I can't tell you anything about my comings and goings or about military operations," Lt. Roberts stated, firmly. "I told the boy, Neal, Pendleton is not on our agenda. That is all I can say. I am merely a scout and runner. I do not read the written orders I carry from one bivouac to another, I just deliver them."

"How long have you been in the army? Is your father fighting, too?" Mandy tried another tack.

"No. My folks are both dead. My pa was killed at Manassas. My ma died of a broken heart about six months later. I'm their only son, born late in their marriage. That's why I volunteered to scout. If I die there's not much loss. Our farm in southern Pennsylvania was burned to the ground by the gray coats and all our livestock taken. I was in my second year at a local college. It just seemed natural to leave and join the army. All my worldly goods I carry with me; thirty years old and my material wealth is small enough to fit into a saddle bag…" His voice, tinged with bitterness and regret, trailed away as he put his hand into his pants pocket.

"Here is a picture of my ma. She was a wonderful woman: smart and strong and not afraid to work right along side her man. I miss her. It was from her I got most of my learning, both spiritual and secular."

Mandy studied the faded picture. The woman looked rather plain but the set of her jaw suggested resourcefulness and her eyes shown with wisdom. "A lovely picture," Mandy murmured. "I can see that your facial features are like hers, also." She studied his face for a moment taking in the square jaw, generous mouth, slightly hooked nose, straight blond thick brows and high forehead." He was not of great height but the rippling muscles under his shirt suggested a lifetime of hard physical work. Really, he was quite pleasing to the eye, she thought.

"You have been so kind." Lt. Roberts took Mandy's hand is his. "An angel could not have been more caring. It seems my good deed of the squirrels has come full circle. I thank you from the bottom of my heart."

Mandy searched his face for duplicity but found instead the clear, steady gaze of a man who meant what he said. By far his best feature was his bright blue eyes that seemed to look right through her. There was an aura of raw strength about him yet at the same time his long, tapered fingers suggested a sensual, artistic side as well.

"It was reckless of me to wear my uniform jacket," Lt. Roberts said. "I put it on for an important rendezvous during the night. I was just about to remove it at daybreak when I was shot. Someone probably thought they were doing their neighbors a favor.

"Forgive my boldness, but tell me about yourself. You do not have the local accent. An interesting story will help pass the time." He took a bite from the apple Mandy had brought, shifted his body so he was leaning on his good arm and waited expectantly.

"I'm not sure how interesting my story is, but you are right, I'm from Tennessee. My pa died when I was five and my ma married another man who was terribly cruel to both of us. He worked us day and night on his miserable farm. One day he and my ma began to argue and next thing I knew he had pushed her off the porch. She hit her head when she fell. She seemed all right for a few days then took to her bed and died. I left soon after, making my way to Pendleton in search of a cousin. I didn't find her but another family, the Gibbes, eventually took me in after I had worked at the Woodburn plantation for a while. When the Gibbes moved back to Beaufort, I went with them and found a cousin living in Charleston. I stayed with her a while but she died in the flu epidemic of 1855. However, she left me her rental house and a small monthly inheritance. God made it plain to me that I was to care for some of the children orphaned by the epidemic, which I am doing. When the fighting threatened Charleston, I brought my family here in the hope it would be a safe haven. So here I am, blest with good friends and a roof over my head. God is good." Mandy smiled absently, her mind filling with misty memories.

"What an unusual life you are leading. I envy your knowing your calling in life. I am still searching. Ever since I was a child I've had a hunger to know and please God. I remember a scripture in Jeremiah that says, 'If with all your heart you truly seek Me, you shall ever surely find Me, saith the Lord.' I believe eventually I will have a better understanding of spiritual events and will find my place in His great scheme of things."

"I'm sure you will. God never turns anyone away who is seeking Him. I will add my prayers to yours. Now I must hurry home before anyone misses me. Neal will bring you breakfast and extra supplies in case you do decide to resume your duties. However, it would be best if you waited until your wound is completely healed. Should you fall and reopen it, the bleeding will start all over again. Take care and stay out of sight." Mandy gathered the soiled bandages, stuffed them into her carrier and disappeared into the woods.

Lt. Roberts stared after her for a long while then drifted into a deep sleep. In his dreams she appeared to him again dressed in a long, white, flowing gown. "Angel," he muttered in his sleep. "My angel."

The next morning when Neal arrived with supplies there was no sign of the soldier. The lean-to had been dismantled, the branches scattered about, the flattened grass had been straightened and to the unpracticed eye there was no evidence that Lt. Roberts had ever existed.

Chapter Seven

As Mandy set out the breakfast fare the next morning the sky darkened and soon a violent thunderstorm blanketed the area.

"I'm scared," whimpered Lizzie, clinging to Mandy's skirt. "Will we get hurt? Will a tree fall on us?"

"Hush, Lizzie. You're safe here. There are no big trees hanging over this building and besides, the carriage house roof is very strong. It will hold up to any storms that come our way. Come have your breakfast. Nothing bad is going to happen. We need the rain to keep the grass green and the crops growing well." As Mandy helped the little girl onto her chair the front door opened with a bang.

"Sorry to interrupt your breakfast but Lynette needs your help, Mandy. Please come right away." Smith stood on the threshold, a stricken look on his face.

"Beth, you and Katie handle breakfast. I'll be back as soon as I can," said Mandy as she hurried after Smith into the driving rain. By the time they arrived at the main house they were both dripping wet but Smith paid no heed to their situation as he impatiently drew her aside.

"Miss Maude died in her sleep last night," he said. "Lynette is beside herself with grief. Could you sit with her for a while and help with the necessary preparations of the body? I am on my way to notify Rev. McMahon and post a notice in town. I'll stop by the doctor's office, too. We'll need a death certificate. What with this hot weather, we'll have to have the funeral this evening. Thank goodness there are no immediate relatives far away that have to be notified."

"I'm so sorry, Smith. Miss Maude was such a loving person. She was so retiring I never did get to know her very well. She rarely ever attended a dinner or function when we were present."

"True. She kept to herself, spending most of her time with the children. Rose Ellen was her favorite. I'm glad she lasted long enough to see baby DuBois. The last few weeks she has spent hours rocking and cuddling him. Perhaps she suspected her earthly life was coming to a close. She was so accommodating, we often forgot she had a weak heart." Smith wiped his wet face on his rain-dampened shirtsleeve. "Please see to Lynette. She's in the third door on the left at the end of the hall. I must be on my way."

Mandy tiptoed down the long hall, her mind crowded with the painful memories of her own mother's death. There had been little comfort for her then. Her stepfather, Jeb, had dug a hole near a hemlock tree, bundled the dead body into an old quilt and buried his wife as one would bury a livestock animal. Instead of words of scripture, he cursed her for being a weakling and abandoning him. Mandy was allowed an hour to grieve then he ordered her back to the fields. Secretly, she had placed an old crock on the grave, filling it with wildflow-

Mandy's Carriage House Saga

ers and pretty weeds when she could.

As she stood before the closed door she could hear Lynette's sobs coming from within the room. Lord, help me to be a comfort, she thought, then after knocking softly, she entered and knelt beside the grieving woman who was seated on a small chaise, holding a sodden hankie to her eyes.

"Oh, Mandy, whatever will I do without Mother?" Lynette cried. "She was my best friend and confidant. She helped me make all the household decisions and guided me in raising the children. I don't think I can go on without her." Lynette sobbed even louder. "Her wisdom enabled me to approach all life's difficulties with confidence. Now Smith will find out what a fainthearted, scatterbrained woman he married."

"Lynette, I've seen the way Smith looks at you. He would love you devotedly no matter how many personality quirks you had. Perhaps he longs to be your best friend and guide but has been reluctant to step between you and your mother. Try leaning on him; his shoulders are very broad. In any case, he has dedicated his life to caring for you and the children. Take comfort in that." Mandy placed an arm around Lynette's shoulder.

"I do. I'm sorry to be such a baby. Mother had not been feeling well this past week, but I never dreamed she would die so soon. I didn't even get to say good-bye!" The sobs came ever more strongly, racking her grief-stricken body.

"You can say good-bye now, Lynette, as we bathe and dress her. By noon people will be coming to pay their respects. You must be ready for them. Show me which dress you want your mother laid out in." Mandy rose, gently taking Lynette's hand and leading her to a large walnut armoire.

"Mother's favorite dress was the slate gray. She said the color enhanced her eyes. Would you please get me some warm water? I want to care for her myself." Lynette's weeping receded into little sniffles as she laid out her mother's attire.

"Of course." Mandy closed the door softly and made her way to the kitchen where Hannah was busily beating a bowl of eggs.

"Miss Mandy, dis house goin' be upside down fo a while. Best you comes to visit when youse can. I'se de only one left to hep de Mistress. I'se fixin' some cakes fo de folks what come callin'. Iffen youse could stay, I shur be obliged."

"I'll send Katie as a substitute teacher today. When word of Miss Maude's death gets around not many students will come for the afternoon class, I presume. I'll be glad to help where I can." Mandy poured water from the kettle on the woodstove into a large basin and hurried back to Lynette. Then she ran to the carriage house to work out a schedule for her family. By the time she had returned to the main house Lynette had finished bathing her mother and was struggling, between sobs, to dress her.

"Let me help." Mandy raised the body to a near sitting position and guided the voluminous dress over the woman's head. In a few minutes they managed to smooth her hair, powder her face and apply rouge to her cheeks and lips. Lynette brought a satin sheet to cover her from the waist down making Miss Maude look as if she were enjoying an afternoon nap.

"Asleep in Jesus," murmured Lynette. "That's what Mother wanted on her tombstone. Asleep in Jesus. Such comforting words. No more pain or sorrow, only the promise of a glorious new life in God's presence. I envy her a bit, I think."

There was a rap on the door then Smith entered and moved to Lynette's side. "Reverend McMahon will be here shortly. I've fixed a large black bow to the gate to notify passersby of our loss. Is there anything else I can do?" He looked tenderly at his grieving wife.

"I think Lynette would appreciate your just being with her for a few minutes, Smith. I must go change into a more suitable dress then I'll help you prepare for the guests."

"Thank you. Your presence has had a calming effect. I'm eternally grateful." Smith gathered his wife into his arms and gently led her to the chaise.

The rest of the day passed in a blur of somber visitors bringing what meager tokens of food they could to comfort the bereaved family. The LaFarge children, with the exception of Rose Ellen and the baby, stood quietly beside their parents as the line of consoling friends and neighbors passed by. At six o'clock a private family procession led by Rev. McMahon slowly trudged to a clearing surrounded by an ornate wrought iron fence. As the pine casket was lowered into the ground the good pastor cleared his throat and read from the Bible's Book of John.

"'I am the Resurrection and the Life. He that believeth in Me, though he die, yet shall he live; and whosoever liveth and believeth in Me shall never die.' Father God into Thy hands we commit the soul and spirit of Maude Whitten, confident that we shall again see her in Your great city of love where we shall all behold You face to face. Until then bless the LaFarge family with Your everlasting mercy and grace and may their memories of Miss Maude be a consolation to their hearts. In Jesus' name we pray. Amen."

Mandy put her arms around Beth and Katie, turning them away as the sound of dirt clods struck the casket. The heavy silence that followed them home revealed the impact Miss Maude's death had on each child as they relived again the death of their own beloved parents and grieved inwardly.

That night as Mandy tucked Lizzie into bed, the little girl turned to her with a worried expression.

"I don't think Miss Maude is going to like living underground, even if she does have a pretty bed to sleep in," she said. "I don't want to go in the ground either. Why can't we just fly away to heaven?"

Mandy sat on the edge of the bed holding Lizzie's hand. "The pretty bed is just to make Miss Maude's family feel better about burying her, Lizzie. Miss Maude's soul and spirit have already flown away to heaven just as you said. Only her earthly body is in the ground because she will not need it any more. Now she has a new heavenly body that will never get sick or hurt or get old. The Bible says when we see Jesus we shall be like Him. That means we will have a new resurrected body like He has."

"Does everyone go to heaven when they die? I heard the preacher say if we were bad we would go to…." Lizzie paused, unsure whether she should say the word, "You know, to that bad place."

"Only people who have asked Jesus to forgive their sins and have dedicated their lives to Him go to heaven. The folks who turn their backs on God, or ignore Him go to Hell, a place of fire and terrible torment. God doesn't want anyone to go there but some people just refuse to obey God's rules so they have nobody to blame but themselves."

"I'm going to heaven when I die," Lizzie stated firmly. "I want to see my mother and Miss Maude and show them how big I've grown. Do you think my mother is in heaven, too?"

"I'm sure she is. Maybe she is even looking down on you, watching you grow." Mandy picked up Lizzie's doll and placed it on the bed beside her.

"If I see Jesus, I'll sing Him the song I learned in church

last week. Do you think He would like that?" Lizzie began humming the tune under her breath.

"I'm sure He would," Mandy replied, trying to suppress a smile. "Now, close your eyes and say your nighttime prayer."

On October fifteenth, Mandy corralled her group after breakfast. "Put on your nicest clothes. The LaFarge family's mourning period is over and they are having a party to celebrate their new baby. Lynette is quite recovered and baby Dubois is thriving, so all the neighbors are invited to see him. Also, the cotton crop is finally picked and baled and ready to be taken to the gin. There will be music, singing and dancing. A wild boar was caught yesterday and has been roasting in a pit all night. What fun we'll have. For a little while we can forget the miseries of the war."

"Will there be games?" asked Sam, who had been practicing throwing horseshoes. "What about prizes for the winners?"

"I don't know about that. We'll just have to wait and see. Don't go bragging about how good you are at horseshoes, you may end up having to eat crow instead of pig." Mandy smiled at Sam while she buttoned Susan into a pretty pink pinafore.

"Why didn't you tell us about the party sooner?" complained Beth, combing the snarls out of her hair. "Then we could have had more time to decide what to wear."

"That's why," laughed Mandy. "You would have pestered me for days over your hair and clothes, then not have been satisfied. This way your thoughts will soon be on the party and not your attire. You have a vain streak, Miss Beth." Mandy smoothed the young girl's hair back from her face, expertly twisting in tortoiseshell combs to hold it in place. Truthfully, Beth was growing like a weed. The sleeves of her dress ended an inch or more above her wrists and the waist was too high. Somehow, material must be found to make her a new outfit. Mandy sighed. Being a mother had its drawbacks.

"Boys, behave yourselves today. No fighting or teasing the girls. Remember, these are your best outfits and heaven only knows when we will be able to replace them, so be careful."

"We will," they chorused, dashing out the door as the rumble of buggy wheels announced the first visitors.

Katie was the last to be ready. Mandy noticed her meticulous preparations and thought, Katie has turned into a lovely young woman. The checked dimity dress she wore accented all her virtues but was modest enough to suggest refinement. Mandy guessed Katie was beau hunting and ready to pull out all the stops as competition was fierce for the few remaining eligible bachelors.

"You go ahead, Katie, and enjoy yourself for once. I'll tend the children today. Since the party is on home territory they know what they should and shouldn't do." Mandy flashed Katie a knowing look which caused the teen to blush.

"Thank you, Miss Mandy. Come get me if you need help." Katie hurried down the carriage house steps, paused to open her parasol, then regally walked toward a group of young ladies who were fussing over the baby.

"I want to go with Katie," said Lizzie, making a dash for the door.

"Come back here," ordered Mandy. "Katie is with you day and night. Let her enjoy her own friends for a while. Stand still while I button your shoes. I know, let's go see Shadow before we join the party. We'll take him a treat." She ushered Susan and Lizzie out the door and around back of the carriage house.

Shadow was Smith's gray Saddlebred stallion hidden in a special paddock so he would not be appropriated for the war. The only indication he was in residence was the new foal born to the pony mare, Misty, each spring. Mandy herded Susan and Lizzie down the back lane, behind the storage barn and into the woods. Turning left behind a hedge they came to a split-rail fence. A soft nicker from a three-sided shed greeted them as Shadow trotted out to the fence eager for a treat and some petting.

Lizzie climbed the fence with pieces of wild apple in her hand to offer the horse while Mandy scratched his face and tried to untangle his mane. The stallion's ears twitched and his soft eyes gazed at them in a friendly manner. He snorted gently then tried to rub his head against Mandy's shoulder.

"Stop it, Shadow. You'll get me dirty. Poor boy, you don't like being alone, do you?" Mandy rubbed his neck while the little girls patted his shoulder through the fence.

"When I get big, I'm going to ride Shadow, yes, I am," announced Lizzie. "I'll go as fast as the wind. Nobody will be able to catch me."

"Well, be sure to ask Mr. LaFarge first," cautioned Mandy, who could picture the little girl trying to mount by climbing up the horse's leg." Remember, you must use a saddle and bridle. Shadow is too wild to ride bareback."

Susan, meanwhile, had wandered into the fringe of the woods chasing a chipmunk. "Horsie, brown horsie," she said, loudly. Mandy looked in the direction she was pointing. There was someone or something standing in the shadows.

"Susan, come back here and stay with Lizzie. I'll be back in a minute." She hurried into the woods and found herself staring up into the bright blue eyes of Lt. Roberts.

"Richard! How wonderful to see you! What brings you

here? Is everything all right?"

"Miss Mandy, the pleasure of seeing you again would be reason enough to come but I am here to warn you of renegade deserters from the southern army who have begun looting and burning the farms of those folks supporting Jeff Davis. Several places in Greenville have already been destroyed and they may be headed in this direction. It would be wise to post a lookout for the next several weeks. They strike at night, the cowards, and are gone before anyone can identify them. Be on your guard."

"Miss Mandy! Where are you?" Lizzie's plaintive voice could be heard coming toward them.

"Thank you, Richard, for thinking of us. I'll do my best to heed your advice. Please leave before the girls see you. They are too small to keep secrets." Mandy smiled her thanks then turned to intercept the children lest they see the Union soldier.

"Didn't I tell you to stay put?" she scolded as she ushered the children back to the paddock area. "I was just checking out what you saw. It must have been a deer or something. Now, who is ready for the party? I'm sure there will be cakes or cookies to eat. Say good-bye to Shadow and let's join the fun!"

By the time they entered the side garden, the lawn was filled with conversing adults and scampering children. One servant was carrying a tray of liquid refreshment while another followed with a tempting assortment of ham biscuits and fruit tarts. Mandy wandered over to a group of women she recognized as mothers of some of her students. The conversation consisted of complaints about the abject poverty the women experienced daily, and remedies for such problems. Mandy listened carefully. The opinions of the parents

Mandy's Carriage House Saga

often filtered down to the children who had no compunctions about repeating what they heard and saw. If she knew what the latest gossip was, she would be better able to nip it in the bud.

"It is obvious the local people are disillusioned with Jefferson Davis, president of the confederacy," groused Carrie Waters, the hotel chef. "He had promised either no war or a short, decisive victory[1]. Instead, thousands of men have died; taxes have been levied on just about everything except breathing and Confederate money isn't worth the paper it was printed on. A soldiers' pay of eleven dollars a month is the wage paid a slave owner for the use of a slave for the same length of time.[2] The army's morale has sunk like a stone." As she paused for breath, Mrs. Masters jumped in with her litany of complaints.

"I hear many of the soldiers are quitting or taking unauthorized leave in order to plant fall crops and rescue their businesses from bankruptcy. My husband said a cord of wood, which before the war sold for one dollar a cord, now cost thirty-four dollars a cord.[3] Cloth, thread, needles, coffee, sugar and other basics are almost impossible to purchase although it is rumored that storekeepers are hoarding these items long after they profess them to be out of stock."[4]

"We've nothing more to give to the cause. Our church has tried to collect food and clothing to help some of the soldiers' families but you can't get blood out of a turnip," said Mrs. McMahon, a local pastor's wife. "The sad part is this war is so unfair. The wealthy men pay less fortunate men to fight in their place. I've heard my husband say it's a rich man's

---

[1] Edgar, South Carolina, A History; University of SC press, 1998 P.362
[2] Edgar, South Carolina, A History; University of SC press, 1998 P.369
[3] Edgar, South Carolina, A History; University of SC press 1998 P.369
[4] Edgar, South Carolina, A History; University of SC press, 1998 P.368

war but a poor man's fight."[5]

"Perhaps we should be thankful the actual fighting has passed us by. When I was in Charleston, the effects of the war were all around us. The tension was terrible. It's a blessing being in a small town that is of no interest to the Yankees," remarked Mandy.

A laughing chain of children playing crack-the-whip snaked by her, interrupting her thoughts. She smiled at their carefree joy and walked to where a group of teen girls were admiring the new baby. Mrs. LaFarge stood protectively nearby talking to several of her friends.

"What a terrible time for the cotton gin to break down. Smith is trying to make arrangements to deliver the cotton to a gin in Aiken by traveling in a caravan with several of the other farmers. He believes there will be safety in numbers. I'm afraid for him. These days you just aren't sure who is your friend and who is your enemy," she said in a worried voice.

"Poverty and politics are poor bedfellows," replied Mandy. "When a man can't afford food and clothing for his family his ego suffers terribly. Does Smith think there are marauding gangs nearby?" She wanted to have Richard's report confirmed or discredited.

"We have heard reports from Greenville and Columbia that disgruntled soldiers are looting the fields and farms of Davis sympathizers," Lynette answered. "Of course most folks in this area claim to be neutral. There was a big bruhaha when our state left the Union but now most of our citizens are all pulling for the confederacy, just not as it is today led by Jeff Davis."

---

[5] Edgar, South Carolina, A History; University of SC press, 1998 P 370

"How does Smith feel about Jeff Davis and the Confederate Council?" asked Mandy, taking advantage of Lynette's willingness to talk of family matters.

"He wasn't in favor of the war in the first place. Not that he favors the North, but he felt a certain amount of industrialization would gradually filter down to this area and eventually we would incorporate it into our lifestyle. For example, the cotton gin has been a real blessing. So much time is saved that the people who used to clean the cotton by hand now work at other jobs. We both feel that slavery is a necessary evil but you know we treat our people kindly."

Mandy nodded. Smith treated his people as fairly as possible, even consenting to let the children of the household help be taught to read and write. "Do you think it would be wise to post a guard at night for a while, just in case?" Mandy asked, trying to find the words to encourage Lynette to discuss the issue with Smith without seeming too anxious. The carriage house stood several hundred feet behind the main house and would be an easy target. She feared for the safety of her children.

"I don't know," pondered Lynette. "We haven't heard of anyone in the area coming under attack. This town is not as progressive as Greenville in either thought or substance. Still, it's better to be safe than sorry. I'll mention it to Smith."

"I'm sure Neal would volunteer for a night watch. I will, too. Missing a few hours sleep is inconsequential compared to what might happen."

"True. Let us hope my suggestion is not seen as the wild imaginings of a fearful woman. If men would only pay attention when we wives have intuitive thoughts, life would roll along much smoother. Excuse me, Miss Mandy, I must continue my hostess duties." Lynette gracefully made her way to where several elderly ladies were sitting in the shade. After a few moments of conversation and seeing that each woman had a glass of refreshment she disappeared among the crowd.

Mandy stood to one side watching the social interactions of the people. They displayed such grace and dignity. Although it was obvious some discussions were intense, self-control and consideration of others' opinions kept the speakers on their best behavior. She felt proud to be a part of such a refined society.

"Is it time to eat yet?" Neal asked, running up to Mandy.

"Neal! Where have you been? Your trousers are soaking wet and speckled with mud." Mandy's voice was tinged with exasperation at the sight of his disheveled appearance.

"I took the neighbor boys down to the creek to see the beaver dam. Matt bet me I couldn't walk a small log out to the center of the dam. I thought I could, really I did, Miss Mandy, but the log broke in the middle and I fell into the creek. It wasn't deep or anything. I'm sorry I got so dirty." Neal scuffed the ground with a wet shoe in embarrassment.

"Neal, as the oldest, you are supposed to set the example for the other children. How many others have wet clothing?"

"None."

"Good. They are wiser than you. Now, listen carefully. Lt. Roberts is in the area and warned me about marauders that have been working mischief at night: burning barns, stealing livestock and scaring people half to death. I am concerned about our safety because the carriage house sits back away from the main house and strangers may not know the second floor is occupied. I think a guard should be posted at night. I want you to mingle among the men and listen to their conversations to see if any of them know where the latest destruction has been. If the deserters have wreaked havoc in

Greenville perhaps they will come to Pendleton next especially since so many Low Country residents live here. I may be inviting trouble, but men with a grudge to settle can be very dangerous."

Neal nodded. "I've already heard talk of the trouble. Sam McGee's uncle has a place on the Lower Saluda River that was attacked a week ago. They burned his barn and set fire to his fields. Why would they do that? We hardly have enough to eat and wear as it is. Sam McGee said it wasn't the Yankees but some of our own soldiers doing the damage. I don't understand; they are suppose to be helping us, not hurting us."

"Sometimes it's hard to know just who the real enemies are in life," replied Mandy. "That is why it is so important to put your trust in God and pray for wisdom and discernment. However, I think it would be wise to take turns as sentries at night: you, John, and I. Oh, when will this wretched war end? There seems to be no end to the human misery!" Mandy gave Neal's shoulder an affectionate squeeze then hurried to where Susan was crying loudly.

"What happened? Oh dear, you've been stung by a bee on your finger. Let's go make a mud pie, that will help." Mandy lifted the little girl into her arms and hurried to the well for water. After dabbling in the red clay for a few minutes Susan pronounced her finger all better and ran off to play.

If only all of life's hurts could be resolved with a mudpack, thought Mandy, waving her freshly washed hands in the air to dry.

The celebration reached a climax as the roasted pig was brought up out of its pit of coals. The smell of hickory-flavored pork filled the air. Smith deftly split the now brittle pig's skin and began slicing large hunks of meat from its haunches. Soon he was surrounded by wide-eyed, hungry children anxious to chew on a piece of the crisp skin. The servants quickly brought large containers of vegetables, biscuits and sweet potato pie. For a little while people buried their troubles as they feasted with family and friends. Mandy thought the sweet hickory flavored meat the best she had ever eaten and went back for seconds.

Chapter Eight

By week's end a night watch schedule had been perfected. Mandy stood guard until one in the morning, then Neal until four and John until daylight. In order to make up for lost sleep Mandy napped during the dinner hour. The boys caught a few extra winks whenever they could.

To complicate matters, Smith left to lead a caravan of eight wagons of cotton driven by various neighbors to a cotton gin just north of Aiken. While he was gone Neal and John took over his farm duties, adding to their exhaustion.

One night, when Mandy checked on them in the wee hours of the morning, she found them sleeping instead of keeping guard.

"You boys have too much work to do right now to spend half the night awake. Katie and Beth will take your place every other night so you can get some rest. It has been so peaceful perhaps I'm acting like a silly old spinster." She made a stern face then crossed her eyes, sending the boys into fits of laughter. She, too, was feeling the effects of rationed sleep: her thinking was fuzzy and she had a hard time concentrating on teaching her pupils. Several times she had almost fallen asleep during reading class.

"If there are no reports of further raids by the end of next week, we will turn the whole matter over to the good Lord and resume normal habits. Until then the girls will help."
Standing guard was boring and uncomfortable. Although it was mid-October, the nights still held hungry mosquitoes torturing the flesh. Mandy decided to end her nocturnal watches when Smith returned if he had not heard of any further episodes of looting and burning. Until then she would tough it out, just in case.

Two evenings later, as she kept guard, she felt an uncertain fear deep in the pit of her stomach. It was a chilly, overcast night made more terrifying by the lack of moonlight. She could hardly see her hand in front of her face. The high whine of the crickets grated on her nerves and shut out almost every other sound. Suddenly the cry of a whippoorwill cut through the air. Mandy stiffened in anticipation. It was late in the season for these birds to be calling.

"The rebels are three miles down the woods trail and headed this way," spoke a voice out of the darkness. "Alert your menfolk to prepare for an ambush. I'll be hidden in the shadows to help."

"Thank you, Richard. God bless and keep you." Mandy jumped to her feet to rouse Neal and John. Running to their bedroom first, she roughly shook Neal awake.

"Strange soldiers are coming! Neal, you alert the servants at the main house. John, wake the field hands but tell them

Mandy's Carriage House Saga

not to light any candles. I'll have Katie and Beth take the children downstairs and hide them inside the covered carriages. Hurry, now. Don't light any candles. We want it to look as if everyone is sleeping."

After seeing to the girls, she ran outside to organize some of the farm hands.

"Raiders are on their way here by way of the woods trail. Take some of your best men and head them off," she ordered Tomas, the leader. "The boys and I will stay here in case they elude your attack. Try to stop them anyway you can. Leave two men here to protect Mrs. LaFarge and the children. Quickly now!" Mandy stationed Neal and John in the shrubbery surrounding the carriage house, then stood behind a large oak tree bracing her gun on a rough area of bark. She was so scared her breath came in gasps and the rifle vibrated in her hands. She wasn't sure she could even fire it at a person, but perhaps just the sound of the discharge would be enough to deter the troublemakers.

A few minutes later a gunshot rang out, then another, and another. The air resonated with men's shouts and horses' whinnies. Mandy strained to see what was happening but the darkness was like a solid wall. Then, silence. Still she dared not move until she heard some words of assurance.

"It's over," Richard said, so close to her she jumped in fright. "Three were shot, two escaped. Hopefully, we caught the leader. I doubt we'll have any more trouble. Gather your brood and go back to bed."

"We might just as well churn butter or split wood. There'll be no more sleeping tonight. The children are too excited and nervous. Thank you, Richard. You have saved our lives. We will never be able to repay you. God has surely sent you to be our guardian. I'm sure Mr. LaFarge will want to reward you when he returns from Aiken. Do you want me to tell him of your existence? Perhaps it might serve to protect you from a bullet by a local resident." Now that the danger was over, Mandy prattled on, releasing her stress.

"Do what you think is best. In any case, I will not rely on their good favor but on my scouting skills and intuition. Mankind cannot be trusted to do the right thing in war or in peace. My life is in God's hands. Good-bye for now, Miss Mandy, I will see you again." There was a rustle of branches as he disappeared into the night.

"Neal, John, it's all over." called Mandy. "Go tell Mrs. LaFarge all is well. I'll fix a snack. All this excitement has no doubt made everyone hungry. Put your weapons back in their places. We don't want Lizzie or Susan to find them." Mandy opened the carriage room door and shouted, "Everyone out. All is well. We can go back to bed now."

The children tumbled from their hiding places with everyone talking at once. Mandy let them ramble on as she ushered them up the steps to their living quarters and set a pitcher of mint tea and some scones on the kitchen table. She replied to their questions that it had been so dark she had seen nothing. Nor did she mention Lt. Roberts' part in the affair. Someone, somehow, had been alerted she said, emphasizing the fact they were all safe and no damage had been done.

Long after everyone was again sleeping Mandy lay wide awake, her mind racing. It was evident Lt. Roberts was looking out for them. He seemed to turn up weekly. Perhaps he had varied his route so he passed the farm more frequently. Well, now the score had been evened. She had rescued him; he had rescued her and her family.

"Thank you, Jesus, for Your protection. Put angels around Lt. Roberts to keep him in all his ways. Keep Smith safe as he travels home and help him to accept Lt. Roberts as a friend. Please end this terrible war, even decent men are turning sour." She turned on her side and slept, waking often as scenes of war and devastation invaded her dreams.

The evening after Smith returned, he knocked on the carriage house door. "It's time we had a talk," he said, when Mandy appeared in the doorway. "Please come to the library room as soon as you can."

As Mandy climbed the steps to the main house, she tried to organize her thoughts. How much should she tell? She did not want Smith to think her sympathies rested with the Northern army even if she did disapprove of slavery. What would be the best way to explain her relationship with Lt. Roberts? Perhaps she should emphasize Neal's friendship with the soldier instead. Lynette met her at the door and together they walked into the library where Smith was busily writing in a ledger.

"Thank you for coming so promptly," he said, closing the book. "I understand you took it upon yourself to guard the farm in my absence and your dedication prevented a terrible tragedy from happening. Had I known what you were doing, I would have forbidden it, so I guess I'm happy I didn't know. How did you find out the rebels were coming? Tomas said they were still a half-mile away when they were apprehended. Surely you could not have heard them. Are you clairvoyant?"

"Absolutely not! Those who practice witchcraft are under a curse from God! Let me tell you a story, the story of a modern-day Good Samaritan by the name of Neal." Mandy related the incident of the wounded Yankee soldier and his occasional visits, ending with Lt. Roberts' warning about the marauders. "Now we are even; a life for a life, so to speak. I doubt he will trouble himself about us now that his debt has been paid." Mandy spoke about him as indifferently as possible.

"I would like to meet this man," mused Smith, toying with his ink pen. "Oh, never fear, I have only the greatest admiration for him. His secrets are safe with me. As a matter of fact it would be best if we met at night behind the stables. I would not like to endanger him in any way. I just want to personally thank him for protecting my family."

"Miss Mandy, do you have any feelings beyond simple gratitude for Lt. Roberts?" Lynette asked, cuing in to the softness in Mandy's voice when she spoke of the soldier.

"Why no, I don't think so. We did enjoy conversing together but I….oh, dear, I'm not sure how I feel about him. However, he has not given the slightest indication…" Mandy's voice trailed away in confusion as Smith interrupted.

"When the war is over there will be plenty of men anxious to marry and begin life anew. Your education and abilities will attract many a proper Southern gentleman. Men like Lt. Roberts live their lives on the edge of civilization and do not care to be burdened with family responsibilities, they seek only excitement and danger. Besides, being a Yankee, he has no concept of the intricacies of our culture. You will be happiest with a gentleman who has been reared in the Southern tradition. I have a cousin who plans to visit soon to learn of farming conditions here and bring me news of my family. When he arrives you will meet a fine gentleman, cultured in every way and suitable for you. Until then it would be best if you kept your emotions under control and concentrated on teaching." Smith stood, indicating the conversation had ended.

"Go back to your family, Mandy. Thank you again for your initiative and wisdom. I thank God daily for His leading you to us. You skills and initiative are an inspiration to us all.

Mandy's Carriage House Saga

Good night."

"Good night. I will consider what you have said, Smith. I know you have my welfare at heart. Thank you." Mandy rose and walked briskly down the hall and out the door. She would follow God's plan for her life and no other, regardless of the suggestions of friend or foe, she decided. Southern traditions, indeed! So far much of her life had been entrapped by traditions. If it hadn't been for the war, she would not even be able to work in a vegetable garden. Try as she might, she just did not have it in her to be the household ornament Southern women were expected to be. If anything, the difficult times that had come upon them had only served to prove how strong and courageous women of the South were capable of being. She doubted they would ever again desire to be just an elegant adornment for the male ego.

In her heart she was attracted to Lt. Roberts, but she wasn't sure if it was because of his vulnerability when she was nursing him, in gratitude for his solicitousness, or because they were soul mates. They both had a wild streak in them.

"Lord Jesus, I put the decision of marriage into Your hands years ago. Remind me, dear Lord, to leave it there. I'll not end up a love-sick puppy. What will be will come from Your hand. But Richard is a lovely person: brave, loyal, considerate, kind. Please take that into consideration." She smiled softly as she walked back home.

"Miss Mandy, I don't feel so good," said Alex, the next morning at breakfast. Mandy looked at his bright, feverish eyes and laid her hand on his forehead.

"You have a fever, Alex."

"My arms and legs have red spots on them, too," he replied, holding out an arm for examination. "I feel achy all over."

"I think you had better go back to bed," Mandy said. "I'll fix you some willow bark tea and make a poultice for your spots."

Alex stumbled to the bedroom without a word of protest confirming her suspicion that he had more than just a 'summer complaint'. She had never seen such symptoms before and was unsure how to doctor him.

"Best stay away from Alex for a while," she told the other children. "I'm not sure if what he has is catching. You boys can sleep in the parlor tonight. Katie, please take my place at the morning session of school and I'll return for the afternoon classes. My lesson plans are on my desk. Keep the children busy reciting and reading. If things get too out of hand, send them home."

Mandy gathered a knife and a reed basket and headed to the creek where several large white willows bent their graceful branches over the life-giving water. How thankful she was to have learned so many medical remedies from Soaring Hawk. How long ago her adventure seemed. She had only been thirteen, then. Now she was twenty-six. Where had the time gone?

Ever since she had committed her life to Jesus, her outlook had become more positive. She regarded herself as a person of worth because He lived within her. "I can do all things through Christ, Who strengtheneth me," she quoted from Philippians 14, then added another favorite verse from Psalm 113, 'He maketh the barren woman to keep house and to be the joyful mother of children.' Thank You for all my children, Lord. Look now upon Alex and heal him please, for You are a God Who heals."

After gathering some of the inner bark of the tree, she brewed it in boiling water and took the tea to Alex who lay listlessly staring out the window.

"Here, drink this while I tell you a story." She sat on the edge of his bed and recited the story of Daniel whose faith in God's protection was tested in a den of lions.

"Do you think God is testing my faith, Miss Mandy?" asked Alex. "Does God make people sick so He can test them?"

"Of course not, Alex. God loves His children. It is not His intention to make you sick so He can turn around and heal you. You are sick because of something you ate or for some other reason. Maybe you got the rash from a poisonous weed. Fortunately God made our bodies to heal themselves from most damage. You rest and eat well. I'm sure you will be better in no time."

Three days later Alex still had not improved. If anything, his joints had become stiffer and his fever more intense. Thankfully none of the other children had come down with any symptoms leaving Mandy to deduce the sickness was not contagious. Alex patiently endured all her doctoring but it was obvious his condition was deteriorating. Finally in desperation she sought the help of Maum Opal, an ancient Negress who was known for her healing concoctions.

"Dis here come from a tiny bug bite," she said, staring at Alex. "Mostly, people don die, they jest stay sickly for a long time, den dey die. No one knows de secret fer healin' dis sickness."

Mandy bit her lip and scowled at the bad news. She pressed a penny in Opal's hand and thanked her for her help. Perhaps humans did not have a solution but the Almighty could do anything. She climbed into a covered phaeton and prayed long and hard. That evening she assembled the whole family around Alex.

"We need to pray for Alex's healing," she said. "Each one of you pray as you feel led. The rest of us will agree with you silently. Let's hold hands."

"Dear God, please heal Alex. Take away his fever. Amen." said Neal. John and Sam echoed his sentiments. It was Susan who set the example for the rest of the family.

"Jesus, You are the bestest person I know. You healed my dolly once and you healed a kitty with a sore leg. I know You can heal Alex. If you will make him all better, I promise not to be a bad girl ever again. Amen." Several snickers escaped from John before Mandy's stern look settled him down. She, too, was laughing silently, not at Susan's simple faith but at her bargaining with God. Out of the mouths of babes, she thought. I must teach them that God can't be bought. His gifts come from His overflowing grace and His mercy falls on the just and the unjust. It is impossible to sway God through our works; He delights only in our obedience.

The next Saturday, Mandy awoke to childish giggling and a general commotion. Wrapping herself in her wool bathrobe she ambled into the kitchen to find the table decorated with wild purple asters and joe pye weed. Several packages rested at her place.

"What's this all about?" she asked innocently, pretending she had forgotten it was her birthday.

"Happy Birthday!" everyone shouted as Katie, Neal and Beth carried in platters of pancakes, toast and scrambled eggs.

"Oh my! What a feast. Everyone sit down. Let's enjoy this wonderful breakfast while it is hot. Ummmmm! The blackberry syrup is delicious and the pancakes are light as a feather. What talented cooks I have." She helped herself to a spoonful of eggs, afraid to ask where they had gotten enough eggs to scramble. She hoped the neighbors' hen houses had not been raided.

After everything had been devoured, she opened her presents. There was a brown and white muff made from the pelts of several rabbits Neal had caught; a new set of tatted white lace cuffs to dress up her plain blue blouse made by Katie and Beth; and two fancy wooden spoons made by John, sanded by Alex and carved by Sam.

"The wild flowers are from me and Susan," stated Lizzie, importantly. "We got them down by the stables. Susan fell and tore her dress but Katie said not to say anything about it 'cause it was your birthday. You aren't going to be angry with Susan, are you? We were trying to do something nice for you."

"No, I'm not angry," laughed Mandy. "Susan's clothes are worn thru almost to rags since she is the last in line for hand-me-downs. I think you are all very special to remember my birthday. I feel so loved and appreciated. And now, since you did the cooking, I will clean up."

The boys disappeared to go fishing. Mandy cleared the table and washed the dishes while Katie and Beth gathered the clothes that needed washing. November's warm temperatures and low humidity dried clothes quickly. Nevertheless, laundry was a chore no one enjoyed. The sooner it was done, the better.

With lesson plans, teaching, nursing Alex and household duties, Mandy's days became a blur of activity. The few reports they had of the war were not encouraging. It was obvious the North had better supplies and was more aggressive. President Lincoln's proclamation to abolish slavery had caused even more slaves to run away resulting in many plantation and farm fields remaining unplowed and neglected.

Neal became harder and harder to convince that he was needed on the farm. "Miss Mandy, please let me go to the army. Boys younger than me left months ago. There is something even young men like me can do. We can load cannons or haul water for the mules. Please, please, let me join up," he pleaded. Even the ghastly report of hundreds of maimed and dying men left unattended on the battlefields had no effect on him.

"Neal, you are needed here. Smith has no one to oversee the field hands except you. Do you want us to go hungry? The fields will be let neglected if you aren't here to supervise. Besides, John and Sam need you, too. You're the big brother in our family." Mandy tried every argument she could think of to dissuade him, but it was of no use. Two days later she awoke to a note saying he had gone to serve the Confederacy cause and would write when he could. She stared at the letter while her stomach churned in fear. Would she ever see him again?

"I can't believe it!" wailed Katie, upon hearing the news. "Neal is just a boy! He'll be killed for sure! Why would he do such a thing when we need him here to help with the farm?"

"Neal needs to prove his worth," said John. "He told me he wants to work in the hospital and help the soldiers get better."

"Poor Neal. He has no idea the terrible scenes he will see. I wonder if he is strong enough to stomach the pain and misery he will encounter. We must pray for him daily. I hope he realizes that once he joins the army he can't come home when the mood hits him. He is committed for the duration." Mandy shook her head in dismay, then went to massage Alex's stiffened legs. Keeping busy kept her mind off worrisome problems.

The following Sunday was one of nature's perfect days. The trees were a blaze of color. Wild purple asters, golden rod and white daisies dotted the fields, bobbing gently in a light breeze. Mandy took deep breaths of the vintage air while walking home from church and decided a solitary hike would restore her mental balance. Leaving Katie in charge, she changed into an old cotton dress, slipped on a pair of leather boots, threw an old shawl over her shoulders and headed down the woodland road. The crisp rustling of fallen leaves and the scream of a high-flying hawk brought a smile to her lips. I was born a hundred years too late, she thought. I should have been an Indian living my life in the mountains, free to hunt and hike. She walked briskly along the trail, heedless of time or distance, her thoughts bouncing from one topic to another. She prayed for Neal and thought about her home in Charleston. Was it still standing? Was a Yankee officer occupying it as was the case with many of the other large houses? She pictured each room, smiling to herself as she reminisced of happier days with her cousin Caroline, serving tea to various educators and pastors. In her mind's eye she strolled through the gardens, admiring the beautiful camellia blooms and the confederate jasmine trailing among the live oaks. What a blessed time that was; a time of peace and gentility when people went out of their way to be kind and accommodating. On and on she walked, lost in thoughts of a happier era.

The jerk on her dress sleeve startled her and before she could gather her wits, a hand over her mouth and an arm about her waist immobilized her body. Twisting and kicking she struggled to free herself but in seconds she was trussed up as neatly and tightly as a pig on a spit.

"We got ourselves a good'un this time," chortled a bearded man in a deerskin shirt. "Stop strugglin'. Save yer strength, gal, you gonna need it later, that's fer sure."

Mandy turned to look at her captors. There were three of

them: dirty, scruffy, tobacco-chewing derelicts. They looked like mountain men but could have been runaway soldiers. Their cold, expressionless eyes stared back at her. One of the men spit a stream of tobacco juice that landed on her boot causing her to shudder involuntarily.

"Jesus, help me," she prayed silently, standing straight and tall to show them she was not afraid. A filthy rag gag had been stuffed in her mouth. She tried not to swallow the saliva it was creating, instead, she tipped her head so the liquid could run out the corner of her jaw.

"Move!" commanded the oldest of the trio. He gave the rope tied around Mandy's arms a jerk, almost lifting her off her feet. Stumbling to catch her balance, she adjusted her pace to the rhythmic stride of her captors.

After walking several miles, they came to a dense stand of pine where three horses were tied and a heap of cold ashes revealed the remnants of a campfire. Without a word the men mounted. Mandy was roughly tossed behind her captor, landing on a bedroll tied behind the saddle. As the rope on her hands was tied to the cinch ring, the leader snarled," Don't git any idears, gal. Iffen you try to get free, you'll be drug along the ground and we ain't stoppin' to pick you up."

Mandy shifted her weight to a more comfortable position on the bedroll, then grabbed the back of the saddle with her hands. She detested horseback riding but now was not the time to mention it. Just keeping her balance as they trotted along took all her concentration.

Hours passed. It was obvious they were heading west. The woods were dense; the rivers narrow but deep, and the hills steeper with every hour traveled. As darkness enveloped them, the half moon cast no helpful light yet the men moved confidently along a narrow trail. Mandy was in agony; her bladder demanded to be emptied. Finally she could stand it no more.

"I need to pee," she said, speaking through the gag and reverting to her farm girl language to make sure the man in front of her understood her request.

"Whoa up a minute," he said. "The little Miss needs a potty break." Rough hands snatched her off the horse and led her behind a large cedar tree. Mandy did her business, thankful she had worn her everyday bloomers that had a center split specifically for this purpose. She certainly had no intention of removing even one article of clothing in their presence. It felt good to stand. The long ride astride the horse had turned her legs rubbery. She flexed her ankles, marching in place to restore circulation, but before her body could return to normal she was again shoved onto the bedroll to continue her journey.

She could only guess at the commotion her disappearance had caused at the farm. By now everyone would be frantically searching for her; the children scared witless. She hoped Katie and John wouldn't do anything foolish like striking out on their own to find her. Thank heaven Lynette was there to take charge.

The trail was getting rocky and steep. Several times her tired horse stumbled over loose roots and stones. She gripped the saddle harder and tried to stay relaxed so as to keep balanced. Suddenly she noticed a strange, sweet odor permeating the air. It vaguely reminded her of her stepfather's home brewed whisky. As the sky began to lighten she tipped her head to watch the stars disappear one by one. God knew of her predicament and would soon send help; of that she was sure.

By the time the sun began to burn away the morning haze,

they came upon a dilapidated cabin in a small clearing. After crossing a swift running creek, the men halted the horses in front of the cabin door. Mandy was jerked from her perch, pushed into the cabin and plunked on a musty mattress of pine needles lying on the floor near the fireplace.

"Rest up. We'll need you later," the oldest man said as he tied the end of her rope to a heavy andiron holding a large iron pot over a lifeless fire. Totally exhausted, Mandy lay back against the lumpy mattress, closed her eyes and slept.

It seemed she had just drifted off when a rough shake woke her. "Time to git to work. Rick will show you what to do." The tall, skinny man with squinty eyes jerked his thumb in the direction of the front door.

A soft moan escaped Mandy's lips as she rose from the floor. Every muscle in her body ached and the rope around her hands had rubbed raw spots in her skin. Wordlessly, she thrust her shackled hands at him. With a deft twist, Rick released the knot. Gently she tried to rub some feeling back into her fingers.

"I'm thirsty. May I have a drink?"

"Creek's just beyond the door but don't think of runnin'. One of us will have a gun pointed in yer direction every minnit," he said, waving a pistol in her face.

Mandy slowly walked to the creek where she knelt to splash water on her face and arms, then drank deeply of the cool, sweet liquid. A lively gray and white bird flitted above her, catching insects while in flight. She felt as if she was reliving her earlier trek from Tennessee to South Carolina. She would bide her time knowing that when an escape was possible she would be able to survive in the woods.

The water revived her. After satisfying her thirst, she walked to where Rick stood waiting. He seemed to be the boss. His narrow eyes were calculating; his shoulders broad and his scraggly, dark hair hung in greasy hanks over his collar. A heavy beard covered his mouth so she could not see his lips when he spoke.

"This here's a business. See those jugs? They need washin'. Pour a little creek sand into each one, swish it around good then fill the jug with water, swish again and rinse. Make sure you git all the sand out, then set 'em in this here barrow."

Mandy did as she was told. She assumed the jugs were for holding home-brewed liquor. Perhaps the odor drifting through the air was the mash cooking. She hoped she did not have to work around the still, the smell was already upsetting her very empty stomach.

Several hours later all the cleaned jugs were carefully stacked in the homemade wheelbarrow. Silently, she stood before Rick awaiting another task.

"Can you cook?"

Mandy nodded.

"Jake should be back with some meat soon. Do yer best with it. There's flour and lard in the kitchen. Use whatever you kin find to make a meal, we ain't all that fussy." He waved her toward the cabin with a rough gesture.

Mandy entered the dim gloom of the log building. She had hoped for another outside chore but at least kitchen work was easy, or would be once she cleaned up the mess. She searched in vain for a broom or scrub brush. Finally in desperation she fashioned a makeshift broom from several limbs of a short-needled pine tree growing just outside the kitchen window. It was a poor substitute but she was able to sweep most of the dirt and mice droppings out the door. The rest fell between the floorboards.

Next she cleaned the ashes from the hearth and relayed

wood for a fire, then she carried the stew pot to the creek for a scrubbing. By the time Jake arrived with a half dozen squirrels and a small wild turkey she had made some order out of the cabin's chaos. Since the turkey would take the longest to cook, she tackled it first: scalding the bird, plucking the feathers, cleaning the cavity and finally, fastening it to an iron spit. She lit the fire, tossing on a few green hickory limbs to add flavor to the bird while it cooked, and began to skin the squirrels.

She could find no vegetables to stew with the squirrels so with Jake in tow she rummaged along the creek and nearby woods for herbs and mushrooms. On impulse she dug deep into the mud bank of the creek and found a clump of wild leek bulbs. Their garlic-like flavor would make the stew extra tasty.

The rest of the afternoon she spent cooking and cleaning. By chance she came across a small skinning knife that had fallen behind a chest and, by the accumulated dust on it, probably had been long forgotten. Quickly she wrapped it in a scrap of rag and slipped it into her boot.

The smell of baking biscuits brought the men inside. Although the meat was not yet done, they gorged on biscuits and honey, washing everything down with a crock of home brew.

"Yer cookin's passable," remarked Rick, wiping a smear of honey from his grungy beard. "We've got work up the hill but we'll be back before dark. Jake, truss our gal to the hook in the kitchen. She can catch a few extra winks. Bank the fire so's the meat don't burn."

Jake immediately tied Mandy's hands and feet to a chain in the kitchen on which cured meat had been hung. She submitted silently. Perhaps if she could gain their confidence, they would give her more freedom, she thought, and that would make escaping easier. As she sat on the floor, she developed a plan for survival: make herself indispensable by cooking and cleaning, while at the same time be as undesirable as possible. Although she abhorred being dirty, she would keep a disheveled appearance by eating wild garlic, not washing or combing her hair and rubbing herself with stink weed.

"Dear Jesus, please get me out of here. Send angels to take care of the children. Give them the assurance that I am all right and will return safely. Oh Lord, send someone to help me, please, please. Amen." Tears of desperation, which she had kept bottled up while in the presence of the men, now trickled down Mandy's face. Then a quiet voice spoke from deep within her: "I know the plans I have for you, plans for your welfare and not calamity." Mandy's heart quickened with joy.

"The Lord is my Shepherd, I shall not want." The reassuring words of the Twenty-third Psalm flowed from her lips and lodged with surety in her mind and heart. Help was imminent. She could trust God's grace.

She awoke to the smell of burning turkey. Without her ability to turn the spit, the bird was cooking on one side only. Well, that would teach them to allow her some movement about the cabin. Their supper was being ruined.

The sound of arguing signaled the return of the brothers. The cabin door burst open as Jake vented his anger. "Dadgumit! Where's all the smoke comin' from?" he shouted.

"The turkey's burning," said Mandy. "Turn it over. Stir the stew, too."

"I ain't no cook; do it yerself." He gave Mandy a venomous look as he quickly freed her and gave her a shove toward the fireplace. Silently she tended the fire and the food, set the table and at last placed the stew, turkey and remaining biscuits in the center of the table.

"Supper's ready," she said, grabbing a turkey wing and biscuit then retreating to the safety of her mattress to eat. Hungrily she gnawed on the meat, trying to ignore the slurping and belching as the men made short work of the meal. After filling their bellies, they sat out on the cabin steps smoking corncob pipes and chatting.

Mandy cleaned up, stuffing herself with leftover turkey as she worked. She had to keep up her strength so as to be ready to travel at a moment's notice.

That night, instead of tying her to the hook, Jake fastened a handmade chain around her right leg and locked it to a heavy anvil. "That'll slow you down in case you git any ideas," he said with a sneer.

"Yer bed is in the kitchen from now on. I put a mattress under the table, use this for a cover." He threw an old smelly saddle blanket at her. Mandy crawled under the table, adjusted her body to the lumpy mattress and slept fitfully.

At the first bird song, she rose silently to poke up the fire and brew some coffee. Dragging the anvil behind her, she measured some cornmeal into the stew pot, added water and set it over the fire to simmer. As if reading her mind, Rick mumbled from his pallet, "Use the outhouse, gal, but don't try anything stupid."

Mandy grabbed the chain with her right hand and pulled the anvil behind her as she walked. Step, pull, step, pull. It was slow going but she could manage. By the time she returned to the cabin the brothers were up, scratching and snuffling and demanding breakfast.

"Whar's the meat?" asked Clem, the youngest, as Mandy plunked the pot of grits on the table. Wordlessly, she unwrapped the remaining turkey and placed the platter in front of him. In a matter of minutes the bare carcass and empty pot announced the end of the meal. She had eaten nothing and now nothing was all that remained. How could they eat so much, she wondered as she poured them more coffee.

"Yer goin' with us today, missy. Clean up and git yerself ready. We'll leave as soon as we finish our coffee." Jake jerked his head in her direction while taking a huge gulp of coffee. Mandy washed out the stew pot, heaped ashes over the hot coals to keep them alive for the supper cooking and filled an empty crock with water to take along.

It wasn't long before she was back on the bedroll behind the saddle while the horses climbed steadily, twisting and turning around rocks and fallen logs until they reached a clearing where a grassy corral of logs had been constructed. Beyond the enclosure Mandy could see a thin plume of bluish smoke rising with the morning mist. She slid off the horse and stood quietly until Jake gave her a prod.

"See that pile of cut logs? Carry the pieces over to the rick and stack 'em so's they'll be easy to use." He pointed in the direction of the smoke that indicated a working still.

She walked to the jumble of brush and logs, picked up several small logs (she didn't want them to know how strong she was) and slowly walked to the place where Rick had built a rough support. Back and forth she walked, hauling logs and cut branches while the brothers split and sawed larger sections of a fallen tree. By afternoon a rick five feet high and ten feet long had been filled.

Mandy was exhausted. Spurning the offer of liquor which the men nipped on constantly, she had not had anything but water all day. Her legs and arms trembled with fatigue and she was so dizzy she could hardly stand upright. It took all her remaining strength to balance on the horse during the return trip. That is, until Rick began to talk.

"I bin watchin' you fer some time," he said. "You comin' an' goin' to school and workin' around the farm. Yer friends thot we'd bin scared away when they came after us that night but we jist bin biddin' our time. That farm will sure make a fine fire, but first we gots to get the brew delivered. Folks are willin' to pay good right now since they's nothing else available."

Mandy sucked in her breath. These were the men who had planned to destroy Meadow Wood! Her adrenaline surged with the revelation and her determination to escape became stronger than ever. Now she had another purpose, she must warn Smith of a coming attack. Still, she must be careful not to let her captors know her feelings. She must act as if she had given up all hope of returning to Pendleton.

The days passed in a jumble of hard labor. Her vow to ignore personal cleanliness seemed to bother her more than the men, whose body odors, mixed with the liquor smell, turned Mandy's stomach. Every night and throughout the day, silent prayers rose heavenward from her heart. So far no opportunity for escape had presented itself. When she worked she was under constant guard and when she rested she was chained to the anvil. To her calculation it had been ten days since she had been kidnapped. She doubted anyone would find her here; the area was so remote she had not even seen smoke from another cabin anywhere on the mountain or in the valley below.

"God knows where I am. He will send help," she said, gathering up her unraveling faith. She quoted Jeremiah 33:3 'Call on Me and I will answer Thee and show Thee great and mighty things which thou knowest not.' and Psalm 50:15 'Call upon Me in the day of trouble. I will deliver thee and thou shalt glorify Me.' How thankful she was that she had memorized so many Bible verses. They were such a comfort to her now.

There was no doubt being hidden away in the forest was emotionally affecting the brothers. Some days they laughed and worked together in harmony; other moments found them quarreling among themselves to the point of fist fighting or circling each other with knives drawn. When a battle was raging, Mandy withdrew to the kitchen and was as still as a church mouse knowing it would not take much for their liquor-crazed minds to blame her for all their troubles.

On the fifteenth morning of her captivity she awoke with a sense of anticipation. Within her spirit came the knowing that her escape was to be today. It was all she could do to control herself; she wanted to laugh, dance and sing for joy. Instead, she quietly busied herself with the breakfast routine.

"We got jugs to fill today, missy," stated Jake. "Load all these here jugs in the feed sacks. Put the same number in each sack. Be quick about it."

Mandy did as she was told, her eyes down cast. It would not do to arouse any suspicions. As Jake packed an extra horse with the jugs and other equipment, Mandy went into the cabin to bank the fire. Her eyes roamed over the place of her captivity. If the circumstances had been different this would have been a cozy place to escape the summer heat. As it was, she silently said a joyful good-by, anticipating she would never see the cabin again.

Once at the still she set out the jugs while the men prepared to drain the liquor through cloth strainers. As she stacked the filled vessels, an urgent thought came to her that she should move away from the brewing apparatus. Slowly, so as not to draw attention to herself, she took several jugs and walked about fifty feet to the edge of the woods. Suddenly there was a huge explosion. Spewing liquor from the still created a fireball that flared out in all directions. Screams came from the brothers as their liquor-saturated clothing caught fire. In the midst of the chaos, Mandy jumped to her feet and began to run. This was her chance to escape and she was taking full advantage of it! Scarcely had she gone a hundred yards when she heard hoof beats behind her. Instinctively she began to weave in and out of the trees to avoid capture but it was no use. The rider and his agile horse bore down upon her. To her horror, she felt hands clamp on her shoulders. She struggled furiously, determined to free herself, until a familiar voice shouted, "Miss Mandy, stop fighting before my horse runs over you!"

"Richard! Thank God you've found me!" She reached her arms up, grasped his hands and swung aboard the trotting horse, landing askew across the saddle. "Thank you, Jesus! Thank You, Jesus!" was all she could say as she righted herself. Richard's strong arms enfolded her, holding her securely on the saddle. She was safe at last.

"I've been looking for you for over a week," he said as they rode along. "One night in a dream I saw the cabin and the still. I had passed it months ago during a scouting expedition but wasn't sure how to find it again. I finally figured out it was in the north Georgia mountains. Once we entered this section of the mountains my horse seemed to know the trail and brought me right to the cabin. I wouldn't doubt that angels guided him all the way. I've been watching you for two days, trying to figure out how to disable the men while keeping you safe. I followed you to the still and used gunpowder to create the diversion. I don't think those fellows will be making white lightening for a while, if ever again."

"Thank God you took the dream seriously. I'm sure an unseen angel guided your horse because I have been praying day and night to be rescued. Oh, Richard! I'm so glad you found me!" Tears of relief trickled down Mandy's face. It was all she could do to keep from crying hysterically.

"Now, now. You're safe with me. Don't cry." Then he began to laugh. "Mandy, your tears are making white streaks down your face. I've never seen you so dirty, and you stink to high heaven. I suppose you let yourself go on purpose, but if you are to ride with me all the way back to Pendleton, you need to bathe. At the first sign of water we'll stop so you can clean up. I've an extra set of breeches and shirt you can wear until your clothes dry or you can travel wet but either way, bathe you must."

Mandy grinned. "I've smelled rank for so long I'm used to it, but for your sake and mine – lead me to water."

An hour later they heard the boom of a waterfall and found at its base a lovely pool of clear water shimmering in the sunlight.

"Perfect!" squealed Mandy as she slid off the saddle. Laughing and splashing in the icy stream, she quickly scrubbed herself and her clothes clean with a piece of soap supplied by the Yankee soldier. How wonderful the water felt even if it was so cold her teeth began to chatter and her lips turned blue. Again and again she plunged her head beneath the ripples to rinse her hair until it was squeaky clean. Finally she waded ashore, wringing the water from her clothes as best she could, then climbed onto a large boulder to let the sun warm her.

"I feel renewed in body, mind and spirit," she said, sporting a huge smile. "I'll never again allow myself to become this dirty. Truly, cleanliness is next to godliness." She ran her fingers through her hair to separate the strands and fluffed her dress to dry.

"We'd best be on our way. I want to be out of these mountains before nightfall," said Lt. Roberts, wrapping his wool army jacket around her for additional warmth. Next he unwrapped a strip of beef jerky from his pack. "Eat this. It will stave off your hunger pains. When we camp for the night, I'll fix a proper meal."

"Don't bother. I want to go home. A little hunger never hurt anyone. Just fix some coffee or mush when you want to rest your horse and let's keep going. Oh, I can hardly wait for a cup of English tea. Just a simple cup of tea will give me joy for the rest of my life."

They rode until it was so dark the horse began to stumble. Finding a level spot, Lt. Roberts quickly started a small fire and began heating water from his large canteen. "Here. This is from Sam," he said, handing Mandy a carefully wrapped packet. "Sam was so sure I'd find you he gave me some of your favorite biscuits and several spoonfuls of tea. How could I not search until I found you, spurred on by faith like that?"

"Bless that boy. He has such a compassionate nature. I don't know what I'd do without him. I wonder how he found this tea? I had stashed it away for emergencies. Well, hopefully there will never be an emergency greater than this. Oh, this tastes so good! Richard, you are an excellent cook." Mandy sipped her tea from a metal cup and munched on a sweet potato biscuit.

"Don't be sarcastic, missy. I can do more than boil water. Being alone so much in the wilds has sharpened my culinary skills. Someday I'll treat you to woodcock stew a la Richard." He shared her tea and helped himself to another biscuit. "These are downright tasty. That Katie is a fine cook. It's too bad she's so young, she'd make some man a fine wife." He gave Mandy a teasing look.

"I can hardly wait to sample your cooking. Shall we say next week? That is, if you can find enough birds for my whole family. Woodcock are notoriously hard to capture. Are you up to the challenge or do you think God will lead them right into your saddlebags as He did the animals into the ark." She was enjoying their banter.

"I'm afraid the timing is not right, Mandy. The war is coming to a head. Our forces are gathering in Tennessee for a major battle. I'm needed there, but I'll return as soon as possible. I believe the war will soon be over. The Southern army is destitute. How they have managed to continue on this long, I don't understand. They are all heart. General Sherman is planning a major thrust south and if it goes as planned the end will come quickly. Of course, this is all confidential. I trust you will tell no one." Richard's voice grew solemn as he spoke about the turn the war was taking.

"Of course," murmured Mandy, sipping her tea. Who won what battle seemed of little importance to her at the moment; she just wanted to go home.

Chapter Nine

"Miss Mandy's coming! Miss Mandy's coming!" shouted John, who had been picking up pecans near the woods trail. Dashing ahead of the weary horse, he shouted at every ten strides then looked back at the duo to see if they were still following. As he rounded the carriage house, doors on every floor of the main house opened and white and black alike vocalized their welcomes. Katie and Beth dashed down the carriage house steps while Sam vaulted over the railing, landing in a holly bush. Susan and Lizzie, clinging to Lynette's hands, stared wide-eyed at the commotion.

"Oh, my darlings, I've missed you so!" Mandy jumped from the horse before anyone could help her down and gathered as many children as would fit in her outstretched arms. "I'm back safe and sound. I'll never leave you again, I promise."

She glanced up in time to see Smith LaFarge stride across the yard to where Lt. Roberts stood holding the reins of his horse.

"Let me welcome you to Meadow Wood," he said. "I've got much to thank you for, it seems." Lt. Roberts hesitantly shook Smith's extended hand. "Don't worry yourself, man. I've no intention of letting local bigotry interfere with the gratitude I feel toward you for returning this gracious lady to us. Let John stable your horse while you join me in some refreshment."

Lt. Roberts passed the reins of his tired horse to John saying, " Feed him the best you have. It's been a strenuous journey." Then patting his mount's neck, he turned and followed Smith into the house.

Mandy hurriedly thanked Lynette for overseeing the children during her absence, noting Alex was missing from the group, a sure indication of his continuing illness. Gathering her brood, she rushed up the steps and into the room where he sat.

"Alex, how are you? I hoped you would recover while I was gone. Do you feel any better?" She brushed his coal black hair back from his face and peered intently into his brown eyes.

"I'm some better," he replied. "My arms and legs don't ache as much as they did. Where did you go? What took you so long to come back?"

"I've had quite an adventure," she said. "One I don't care to repeat. I'll tell all of you the story just once then I don't want to hear anything about it again. Agreed?"

While Katie brewed Mandy some tea and fixed sandwiches, Mandy told of her kidnapping. She glossed over the whole situation, making it sound like a grand adventure instead of the dangerous situation it had been, emphasizing God's grace and Lt. Robert's rescue. "And now, I'm home again, fit as a fiddle. I must change and go to the main house for a few minutes to bid Lt. Roberts a proper good-bye. I won't be long, I promise."

She quickly dressed in one of her better day dresses, brushed her hair and pulled it back with a satin ribbon, dusted her face with sweet smelling talc, drew on a pair of soft slippers and hurried next door. As she entered the main hall, she met Smith and the Yankee soldier conversing in the hall.

"I've come to thank you again for all you've done on my behalf," she said, breathlessly. "The children also send their regards. Must you leave so soon? Your horse could stand a good rest, I'm sure. Perhaps you would consider staying the night and beginning fresh in the morning."

"It sounds tempting but I plan to leave right after supper. Smith has offered me the luxury of a warm bath and clean clothes, along with some good down-home cooking. After that I must be on my way. I'll stop again when I'm able."

Mandy hid her disappointment by smiling graciously. "We'll be happy to see you whenever you come. God go with you." She retreated to her house, fully aware that Smith, reading between the lines, knew her heart went with the Union soldier.

As word of Sherman's devastating march circulated throughout the South, people in the major cities left their homes and sought refuge in small, out-of-the-way places. Low-country folk who had summerhouses in Pendleton and the surrounding foothills arrived in various states of penury, causing what little food there was to be stretched even further.

One by one the weary Confederate soldiers who had been injured and could no longer fight made their way home. Some arrived minus an arm or leg, the haunted look in their eyes revealing more of the horrors they had experienced than words could ever describe. Wives and mothers joyfully welcomed them with open arms, then in the silence of night, wept bitter tears at the mental and physical brokenness of their loved ones.

In late November, word came that the men in gray had been soundly defeated in Tennessee and chased into the Georgia mountains. Many of these soldiers, half-starved and without ammunition, set up camps in various hidden valleys to avoid being caught and shot for deserting. Looting became their livelihood. Even the smallest hamlet was often stripped of its essentials.

Mandy had received only one letter from Neal saying he had joined a South Carolina regiment near Sumter and had been assigned to haul dead and wounded men from the battlefields to camp hospitals. She shuddered at the grisly sights he must be seeing and prayed he would not be killed by a sniper's bullet.

Lt. Roberts had not visited since rescuing her, adding to her worry. Was he engaged in fighting or had he been killed? She busied herself in teaching her students, pushing them beyond all their expectations.

One afternoon while Mandy was grading papers after school had been dismissed, she heard a light tap on the door. "Come in," she said, rising to greet the caller.

A tall, thin woman dressed in a gray homespun hooded cloak scuttled through the doorway and quickly shut the door as if afraid someone would recognize her. "Miss Greene, I'm Charlotte Collier from the Wild Hog Road area. You are teaching my daughter, Lucy." Mrs. Collier walked to where Mandy stood and offered her hand.

"How nice to meet you at last, Mrs. Collier. Is Lucy ill? She has not been in school recently. Her attendance has been rather sporadic this year." Mandy mentally pictured the thin, painfully shy girl of twelve who always tried to blend in with her surroundings.

"It's my fault she doesn't come regularly. She stays home to tend me and do the housework when I'm not able. May I talk to you in confidence, Miss Greene? I have a need to tell someone my troubles." Mrs. Collier's voice trembled with emotion as she twisted a piece of her cloak between her hands.

"Of course. Whatever is said here will remain here," Mandy replied. "Please sit down. Take your time, I have all afternoon."

Mrs. Collier crumpled onto a bench. "It's my husband. He drinks more than he should. When he's sober, he is very responsible, but when he's drunk, he turns into a beast. At first he just threw things and broke chairs and the like, but this year he has become more violent and has begun hitting me. Three weeks ago he broke several of my ribs. That is why Lucy stopped coming to school. She was doing my work while I recuperated. Yesterday he did this." Mrs. Collier dropped her hood, revealing a swollen brow and dark bruises on her cheek and forehead.

"Dear Mrs. Collier!" Mandy exclaimed in concern. "Have you seen a doctor?"

"I dare not. My husband has threatened to kill me if I tell anyone what goes on at home. The reason I am here now is not for myself but for Lucy's sake. I've seen him looking at her in a dangerous way, if you know what I mean, Miss Greene. Lucy is a timid child, a child of my old age. If something terrible ever happened to her I'm afraid she might become mentally disturbed."

"God help you and keep Lucy safe," Mandy murmured. "What about talking to your pastor. Perhaps he could help."

"I have hinted to him all was not well between my husband and me but he told me it was my Christian duty to endure. He said the Bible commanded wives to be obedient to their husbands." Mrs. Collier began to sob, her shoulders heaving with each breath she took. "Please, Miss Greene, tell me what to do! I have managed to save a little money. Is there someplace far away I could send Lucy? A school, I mean."

"It's not just Lucy. You need to get away, too. Shame on that pastor for misquoting scripture. The verse in Ephesians you are referring to says that wives are to submit to their husbands as unto the Lord. Jesus would never treat a woman the way your husband has treated you. You are not to be a physical outlet for you husband's anger and frustration. Jesus taught that women were to be honored and respected. Perhaps you should have demanded your husband respect you more at the beginning of your marriage. Well, that is water over the dam. Let me think. We'll need to hide you both somewhere he would never think to look and we must do it quickly." Mandy racked her brain but all she could think of was to ask Smith's advice.

"Go home and pack what you and Lucy can easily carry. Come back tomorrow or as soon as you can get away without drawing attention to yourselves. I live in the carriage house at Meadow Wood. Do you know the place?"

"Yes. I will plan to come on Saturday. My husband goes to Anderson on that day for farm supplies and to socialize. When I'm bruised, he makes me stay at home." Mrs. Collier's sobs receded as she began to plan her escape.

"Thank you, Miss Greene. I'm so sorry to burden you with my problems but Lucy said you were a caring person and would help if you could. I hope I'm not putting you in any danger. We will try to disguise ourselves a bit so no one will recognize us." She rose from her seat and again offered her hand which Mandy shook gently.

"We have four days to formulate a plan," replied Mandy. "I'm sure God will show us what to do. Stay safe, Mrs. Collier. I'll see you and Lucy on Saturday."

After supper Mandy sought Smith who was in the library studying the pages of a ledger. "Smith, I need your help," she entreated, closing the door behind her for privacy.

Smith listened intently as Mandy shared Mrs. Collier's story. "I've met Zeb Collier several times at farmers' gatherings. He's built like an ox. A strong blow from him could kill a person. It's too bad he's taken to drink; he seemed likable enough. Probably the stress of the war and its consequences has taken a toll on his finances as it has with all of us." He smiled wryly while waving his hand toward the open book on his desk. Cupping his chin in his hand, he sat in silent thought for a few minutes.

"I've done business this past year with an elderly gentleman, Mr. Stoker, from Brevard, North Carolina. From what he has said, I believe they have a large log cabin in the woods near Pisgah Forest. Their children are grown and gone so there would be room for Mrs. Collier and her daughter. That is, if he is willing to help. I'll send Eli with a letter tomorrow and have him wait for a reply."

"Thank you, Smith. I knew I could count on you. If your plan doesn't work, I know something else will. I feel sorry for Mr. Collier. Hopefully the shock of losing his wife and daughter will cause him to re-evaluate his life." Mandy's mind conjured up the picture of her own step-father drunkenly sprawled in a tattered canvas chair. She gave an involuntary twitch. She had been terrified of his outbursts when he drank.

"Always the optimist, I see. I hope you are right but my guess is it will only serve to make him more bitter and angry.

Regardless of him, we must do what we can to protect the ladies." Smith eyes returned to his ledger, a signal that he was ready to resume his bookkeeping. Mandy took the hint and left quietly.

Mr. Stoker agreed to the plan in exchange for Mrs. Collier's help nursing his wife who had had a mild stroke and was a semi-invalid. They had been looking for a good woman to ease their situation. Lucy would be a bonus.

Saturday afternoon, in the midst of a rain shower, the Colliers arrived, each carrying a small valise. After a brief visit to dry their clothes and fill their stomachs, Eli, one of Smith few remaining servants, whisked them away in a covered buggy. Mandy waved until they were out of sight, all the while praying for their safety and happiness.

As she warmed herself with a cup of leftover tea, she contemplated the intricacies of men and women. What made a person become abusive? Were early signs of instability ignored during the excitement of courtship or perhaps just not understood? She thought of Richard. Did he have hidden weaknesses that would come to light as he aged or struggled with future pressures? Perhaps she was better off remaining unmarried. She already had children to tend and she was capable of providing a living for herself and them. No doubt when the war ended and people's fortunes improved her salary would increase also since Charleston had a much higher wage scale than Pendleton. Perhaps even her inheritance money would be available again.

Still, there was a deep yearning inside her, a void, really, that demanded to be filled by the love of a man. She wanted a companion and lover, a husband to share all of life's banes and blessings. She hungered to feel protected and treasured. Somewhere there was a man who would value her as a person, not just regard her as a housekeeper, cook and bed partner. She sighed and looked heavenward.

"I love You, Jesus. We have a special bond that cannot be overshadowed by an earthly relationship. You have satisfied me spiritually by Your Presence and love but, please Lord, if it be Thy will, find me a husband."

May 1865 began with sweet, blossom-scented breezes and warm, star-filled nights. The war had ended in April. Most of the Yankee troops were returning north via an eastern route through Winnsboro, leaving Pendleton unscathed so the locals concentrated on planting gardens and reseeding major crops. School had been dismissed as even the smallest child was expected to do his part.

Mandy entered wholeheartedly into the outdoor labors. In a way she was glad most of Smith's slaves had left the plantation. It gave her a chance to do the outside chores that she enjoyed most. Today she was planting beans, squash and melons. The warm sun felt good on her back as she bent over the fertile soil. As she reached the end of a row, a shadow fell over her path. Looking up, her heart gave a leap of joy, for there stood Lt. Roberts, now dressed in civilian clothes and holding a large parcel.

"Morning, ma'am. It's a lovely day for plowing and planting. I've come to pay my respects if you've time to sit a spell." He paused, then grasped Mandy's dirt-stained hand and led her to a small wooden bench under an apple tree.

"Richard! I can hardly believe my eyes! I thought you were dead or had been captured. It's been months since I've seen you. Where have you been?"

"Just doing my job. But now the war is over and I am somewhat free to pursue other interests so here I am." He placed the large bundle into her lap.

Curious, Mandy untied the strings and removed the stained paper. There neatly folded in a stack were three large pieces of material: a blue checked gingham, a yellow floral cotton and a dark green taffeta.

"Oh, my! Will the girls be thrilled to have new dresses! Where did you find such finery? No, don't tell me. I don't want to know. I'll sew these up and rejoice in God's provision. Thank you! Thank you!" She ran the back of her hand lightly over the fabrics and chuckled with delight.

"I also made inquiry about the trunk you left at the Columbia rail station but the whole area had been looted and everything was taken. I hope you had nothing of value stored there."

"No, just clothing, mostly, and a few books. Honestly, I can hardly remember what we did pack we left in such a hurry. I am curious about our house on Glebe Street. We had hidden some of my cousin's valuables in the walls and in the garden. I wonder if the house was damaged by cannon fire or Yankee occupation. The last letter I received from Rev. McMurtry was over a year ago. At that time the house was still intact. As soon as possible I want to return to Charleston and resume tutoring. I still have a year of free rent left."

"Are you unhappy with your life in Pendleton? Could you not begin tutoring here or continue teaching as you have been?" Richard looked at her with concern.

"I enjoy Pendleton very much but there is no immediate future for me here. I have received very little pay, not even enough to rent or buy a house of my own. I'm not complaining; the war effort came first, of course. Nobody has had anything left to give, as it turns out. I'm sure Smith will breathe a sigh of relief when we depart, and so will I. We have been very cramped in those four tiny rooms. The children are growing so quickly they need more elbowroom. I'll admit I'm spoiled. Number Six Glebe St. was so spacious. It will be a joy to have my own room again and a kitchen I can move about in."

"I hate to dash your hopes but I fear the house may have been taken over by carpetbaggers or other undesirables. It would be wise to write to St. Phillips before you journey back. Charleston is not the same as you remember it, Mandy. Many of the wealthy rice planters are now destitute, having lost their fine houses and lands to opportunists including freed slaves and northerners. It's possible many of your friends have fled the area or are living with relatives. I doubt there will be many students needing tutoring right now."

Mandy examined Richard's face to see if possibly he could be jesting but his serious expression gave added weight to his words. Not return to Charleston? Unthinkable! Her cousin lay in Magnolia Cemetery; the Gibbes family was just a half a day's drive away; her friends were almost within shouting distance of Glebe Street.

"I will write to Rev. McMurtry next week," she stated. "Since the house belongs to the Parrish, I can't imagine anyone usurping the property. That would be like robbing God."

Richard nodded. How naïve she was! He had seen the swath of destruction Sherman created. It defied description. Nevertheless, that strategy had ended the war. Otherwise, minor skirmishes may have gone on for years. Now was the time for healing and restoration but as with any society there were those whose greed defied all reason. They were causing as much suffering and deprivation as had the war by preying on widows and the elderly; stealing land, livestock and houses that had been in families for generations. It turned his stomach to see the people, desperate for money, accept a mere token of the real value of their property and belongings.

"I have been hired as a surveyor for the railroad," he said. "As soon as the tracks are laid in this area, we will continue south and west. Since I am familiar with the mountains and beyond, this employment is custom made for me. I would like to continue our friendship while we are both in Pendleton, if you agree."

"Of course, Richard," Mandy replied. "I don't know what I would do without you. Perhaps you could act as a surrogate father for the boys. They need you as much as I do. You could teach them the manly arts, so to speak."

"I'll do what I can. They are fine youngsters. What do your hear from Neal?"

"Nothing. I am beside myself with worry. Surely he would have written or returned by now if he were able. I fear he is dead or mortally wounded. I pray for him daily." Mandy's stomach tightened as she pictured the worst.

"If he were dead probably you would have received a letter of condolence from the government by now. Keep hope alive. Perhaps he wrote and the letter has been lost. I will make inquires as I talk with my soldier friends. Not much gets by them. They are worse gossips than old ladies at a quilting bee." He gave her hand a squeeze, thrilling Mandy to the bottom of her toes. How dear he had become to her. She realized she often tucked bits of daily happenings into the back of her mind to share with him and sometimes longed for his advice on complicated matters. Was this love? She had little experience with positive emotions toward men. Although she no longer viewed them as cruel and untrustworthy, she still continued to withhold her deepest affections from them. She decided to discuss the situation with Reverend Adger, her former employer and friend. How happy she had been when he had returned to the area and moved into Boscobel plantation which he had purchased several years before as a summer house.

"Mandy? Where are you? Am I so boring that you entertain yourself by daydreaming?" Richard's voice expressed the hurt he felt at being ignored.

"Oh, I'm sorry. I do have the habit of retreating within myself when trying to resolve a problem. Please forgive me. You were saying?"

"I was warning you about the small bands of renegade Union soldiers which have resorted to looting the houses and farms of anything valuable. They are determined to return home with as much money and contraband as possible. Of course, you have one of your own, Manson Jolly and his cohorts, doing much the same thing to our occupied forces. I understand he is stealing horses, weapons, supplies, cotton, and anything else not nailed down and selling it in Georgia."

"Yes, I admit that's true. Rumor has it he sets up camp in some of the thickest woods outside Anderson. I guess it must be hard for some men to face the reality of defeat. Vengeance is a terrible taskmaster. I fear for his life."

"And well you may. Not only is he wanted by Federal authorities for shooting Union soldiers making their way home, but by the local lawmakers as well. Please keep watch over your children. Do not let them stray too far from home. Katie, in particular, is becoming a ravishing beauty and would seem a fine prize for some demented soldier."

"I wish Neal were here. He and Katie looked after each other and the younger ones as well. Sometimes I feel a bit overwhelmed taking care of them and teaching, too. In peaceful times overseeing eight lively children was a joy and privilege but today what with the lack of food, clothing, medicine and civil stability there are some days I am almost beside myself with worry." Stop it, she silently chided herself, don't start whining. Men don't like crybabies.

"In those times it is well to remember the words of Psalm 91: 'He that dwelleth in the secret place of the most High shall abide under the shadow of the Almighty. I will say of the Lord, He is my refuge and my fortress: my God; in him will I trust.' Hold fast to your faith, Mandy, God is still in control." He patted her hand gently.

"Thank you, Richard. I needed to hear that. I confess I have not spent enough time reading scripture lately. It's amazing how weak our faith becomes when we do not feed it God's word." There I go again, she thought. I sound so needy.

"True. Our daily bread must be both physical and spiritual in order to be a wholesome person. I will look in on you again next week. I am due in Greenville tomorrow to meet with the railroad developers. Know that I pray for you and your family." Releasing her hand, he smiled down at her, then hurried towards the stable where he had tied his horse.

Mandy remained on the bench, digesting their conversation. She wrapped her arms around herself in an effort to experience a hug but decided it would have felt much better coming from Richard. Folding the paper around the material, she hurried to the house to show the girls their gift from the Yankee soldier turned surveyor.

"Katie, Beth, look what I have for you! New dresses, or rather, soon to be new dresses. Lt. Roberts brought this just for us." She threw open the package on the kitchen table revealing the three pieces of yardage.

"Oh, how beautiful that green taffeta is! Miss Mandy, may I have a dress or skirt from it?" Katie stroked the glossy fabric reverently. "It will make a special party dress. Now that the war is over, some of the families are planning several socials to reacquaint the young people in the area. If I had a nice dress maybe I'd go to at least one of the parties."

"Of course you may have the green. It will look lovely on you with your red hair. I think there is enough to make Lizzie a special dress, too. Beth, you chose next."

"I like the blue check. I just want a nice school dress. Everything I own is too small. Do you think I could have a bit of the yellow floral, just enough to make a blouse? I could wear it with my black skirt. Will you help me make a pattern? I want to try sewing the dress myself." Lately Beth had begun to show an independent spirit that Mandy was trying to nurture.

"Of course I'll help you. Perhaps someone in town has a magazine showing some of the latest fashions. We can copy a style you like. It might be helpful to sew a bit on Susan's dress just to review your skill before you start your own. The small floral pattern is perfect for her. She has outgrown everything, too." Mandy folded the paper carefully over the cloth and placed it in a box that served as a catchall.

"First, we finish the planting, then we sew. The practical side of life must always come before vanity." Gently she pushed the girls toward the porch. " I've wasted at least an hour. Come help me finish the gardening."

The next day dawned sunny and warm so Mandy decided to walk the four miles to Reverend Adger's house. She placed a jar of blackberry preserves in a bag, stuffed soft rags in her almost soleless shoes and began her trek.

The University of South Carolina in Columbia where Reverend Adger taught had closed because of the war. Like Mandy, he had brought his family back to Pendleton where relatives and friends welcomed him home. Mrs. Adger was as missionary minded as her husband and held Bible study every Sunday afternoon on the wide porch of their house. Their workers and neighbors were encouraged to attend. She read and explained scripture then taught hymns and listened to the recitation of memory verses. Since pastors were in short supply because of the war, her efforts and that of her husband were greatly appreciated in the area.

In no time Mandy was walking down the long driveway leading to the white clapboard house. This building was not as imposing as the Woodburn plantation where the Adgers had first lived, but it was a comfortable residence surrounded by large oak trees for shade. From the back porch, looking beyond the vast rolling hills, the blue haze covered mountains could be seen standing silent and strong against the horizon. After a friendly nod to several workers trimming the shrubbery, she climbed the steps and knocked on the door.

"Miss Mandy, as I live and breathe! Come in! Come in! You are a welcome sight. How are you, my dear? I trust our Heavenly Father is looking after your welfare. After all, not a sparrow falls but what He notices it and you are much more important to Him than a bird. Here, sit. Let me get you a drink of water before you begin your tale. Mrs. Adger is giving the children their lessons but will be finished before you leave, I expect." Dr. Adger bustled about making his past protégé comfortable.

Mandy took a deep drink of the cold well water. It was her experience that preachers were never at a loss for words and Dr. Adger was no exception. The next half hour was spent telling her about their garden projects and planned house renovations. Then it was her turn. She had barely begun her tale when one of the workers burst into the room.

"Reverend, sir, soldiers is acomin' up the lane. They's up

to no good, I'm thinkin'."

"Now, Zeke, the war is over. Let us be among those who choose to live in peace. Excuse me, Miss Mandy, while I greet our guests." The tall, burly preacher strode out of the house and stood at the edge of the lawn. Mandy followed him as far as the porch door. A feeling of concern enveloped her as she noticed the rag-tag group of four Union soldiers dismounting and gesturing toward the house. She watched with horror as one brandished a pistol toward Dr. Adger while another took his watch and rummaged through his pockets. Instinctively, she ran to warn Mrs. Adger of the coming danger. In seconds the children were tucked into a secret closet, their study books hidden and the chairs rearranged to make the room look like a library. Mrs. Adger sat on the window seat with embroidery in her lap, looking as unconcerned as possible.

"Sorry to bother you, ma'am, but we are just needin' a few things to make our lives more comfy," said one of the soldiers with a sneer. "First, I'll take your watch, then iffen you'd be so kind to show us where your jewelry is and the silver, we'll just help ourselves and be on our way."

"No need to disturb yourself, my dear," Rev. Adger said quietly, as he handed her watch to the man. "I'll see these soldiers of fortune are well taken care of." Then, leading the men out of the room, he continued, "You men know, of course, you are robbing a servant of God. Are you willing to bear the brunt of God's wrath for your wrongdoings? How much better to repent of your sins and trust the Almighty to provide for your needs." His powerful voice rose to preaching level.

"Shut up," growled one man, pushing the Reverend aside as he knelt down to ransack a trunk. Mandy could hear the clink of silverware as it was dropped into a burlap sack.

"Sirs, the hand of God is upon you!" shouted Rev. Adger,

placing his hands on the heads of the two men riffling the sideboard. "Give me back my watch!"

The men backed away and conferred among themselves then one reached into his coat pocket and produced both watches which he tossed to the irate owner. "Here, we wouldn't want you to be late for your own funeral," he said with a smirk as the others laughed mockingly.

"I beg you to think of what evil you are doing to a people already defeated and destitute. Go home to your families and leave us in peace," pleaded the pastor in vain.

After a few more pilfering efforts, the men returned to their horses, tied their loot to their saddles and prepared to mount. Suddenly a shot rang out. Mandy looked out the window just in time to see one of the ruffians topple from his horse, a bright red stream of blood pouring from his throat.

Rev. Adger rushed forward and held the unconscious man in an upright position. "You men help me get this fellow to the porch. Give me a cloth to press against his wound. Hurry!" He began to unbutton the man's dirty jacket in an attempt to staunch the flow of blood.

Hastily the others dismounted and hurried to examine the injured man. "He'll be dead in five minutes. No use wastin' our time," said the group's leader after peering at the wound. "Looks like his loaded gun musta hit the saddle as he mounted causing it to go off. The bullet went right through his throat. Never seen nuttin' like it. Well, he's got no need for these trinkets, now." So saying, he reached into the dying man's pockets and began pulling out silver spoons, jewelry and other valuables. The other two men cleaned out the pockets on his other side, then tied the reins of his horse to one of their saddles.

"What is his name? I'll see he gets a proper burial," said

Rev. Adger, placing the now dead man gently on the ground. One of the men mumbled a few words then off they galloped.

"Poor soul," said Mrs. Adger as her husband walked into the parlor. "I saw the whole thing from the window. What a tragedy." She stood with her arm about Mandy's shoulders as if to comfort her.

"'Vengeance is Mine, I will repay, saith the Lord.' That's what the Good Book says. Today we have witnessed this scripture fulfilled before our eyes. I'll send for the overseer. We'll bury him in a far corner of the cemetery." Dr. Adger changed his blood-stained waistcoat then went to look for men to help with the burying.

Mandy spent a rather subdued half-hour with Mrs. Adger and the children then decided to return home. Today had turned out far differently than she anticipated and she longed for the normalcy of her own four walls.

That evening she told Smith and Lynette of the marauders and urged them to hide anything of value. For further protection, Smith helped form a group consisting mainly of old men and young lads, to help ward off the small bands of rogue soldiers that came to the area in search of booty. The local women breathed easier knowing there was some form of protection available.

The war was over but peace was still a stranger to the area. Because of these and other adverse circumstances the hearts of the southern people grew hard. Most of them no longer considered themselves to be a part of the United States.

Chapter Ten

Mandy closed her lesson book and stared pensively at the driving rain beating against the schoolhouse window. It was December 10, 1865. She was twenty-seven years old, poor as a church mouse, mother to seven youngsters – actually eight if she counted Neal as a youngster- single, with only an itinerate soldier-surveyor for a beau, and a school teacher whose only salary was room and board plus five dollars a month. It was not exactly the life she had envisioned for herself. To top it off she had received a disheartening letter from St. Phillips Church in Charleston that the house she had rented had been ransacked by Yankee soldiers and was to be sold. So little of her cousin's lovely furnishings remained that it was not worth returning for them, the letter said.

A stray tear trickled down her cheek as she took stock of her life. Her lovely house was gone as were her belongings. The monthly stipend endowed her by her cousin had ceased shortly after she had come to Pendleton due to a run on the Southern banks and her tutoring ability was unwanted because the universities were struggling to rebuild and refurbish before opening to students. Her future looked bleak, indeed.

Then, from deep within her the Holy Spirit whispered these words: 'My God shall supply all of your needs according to His riches in glory by Christ Jesus.'

"Yes, Lord. I know You will meet my needs as You have in the past. And who knows the greatness of Your riches? I suppose they are as wide as the sky and as deep as the ocean. Certainly You have more than I will ever need. Forgive my pity-party, Lord Jesus. It's just that Christmas will be austere again this year because I have nothing to give the children except to make some rag dolls from scrapes of the material Richard gave me and you know the boys aren't interested in toys.

"I'm worried about Neal, Lord. Not a word from him in months. Is he dead or alive? I look at the pinched faces and hollow eyes of my students and feel so frustrated at not being able to cheer them or even feed them. Everyone seems to be struggling and suffering so. When Smith told me Mr. Collier had died in the war and his farm sold, it was just another misfortune among many in our area. Please, Jesus, do something."

She gathered her books, placed them in a worn valise, threw her heavy cloak around her shoulders and went out into the storm. By the time she arrived home she was soaked to the skin and shivering from the cold.

As if anticipating her mood, Katie met her at the door with a hug and a hot cup of sage tea. Mandy eagerly sipped the steaming brew.

"Ummm. I love sage tea. It reminds me of summer days and warm breezes. Thank you, Katie, for being so thoughtful. Where are the others?"

"Down at the stables. We are supposed to join them as soon as you've warmed up and changed your clothes." Katie's voice betrayed her excitement.

What could be going on, wondered Mandy. The pony wasn't due to foal for several months. Perhaps Smith had found a new horse or mule. She hurriedly finished her tea, splashed water on her face and changed into a dry wool dress. She had to trot to keep up with Katie as the young girl practically ran down the path to the stable.

Mandy could hear the babble of voices as they approached the barn. As she stepped inside, the semi-circle of children parted to reveal the object of their excitement. There was Neal, sitting on an old milk stool, dressed in tattered pants and torn jacket, his hair shoulder length and sporting a full beard.

Mandy gasped with surprise and concern. "Neal! Is that you? Goodness gracious! It is you! Thank God you're safe! Welcome home!" She stooped down to give him a hug then hesitated as she noticed his right leg pointing stiffly in front of him. "Are you hurt? What happened? Come up to the house and tell us all about your travels."

"Whoa, Miss Mandy. One question at a time. I'm fine, now. During a skirmish I was kicked in the knee by a horse and now the joint is stiff. It's no matter. I walk with a swagger, is all. The gals seem to like it. It makes me look important." He laughed at his little joke.

"I don't dare come to the house until I've bathed and changed clothes as I fear the lice and other varmints I carry would invade your fine dwelling." He scratched his side as if to emphasize his predicament.

"Katie, boys, hurry and get Neal some hot water. There

are clean towels under my bed. Beth, you go ask Mrs. LaFarge for some of Mr. LaFarge's cast-off clothing: at least some drawers, a shirt and pants. Shoes would help, too."

Everyone scampered to help, leaving Mandy alone with the bedraggled boy. Neal peered into Mandy's eyes, a look of anguish on his face.

"Miss Mandy, please don't ask any questions about the war. I was took prisoner last January and spent the rest of the time in a prison in Pennsylvania. It was horrible! Men died daily from the cold and their injuries. We all had influenza and the trots. I thought I was a goner several times but an old soldier who knew he was dying saved some of his food for me. It probably was the only thing that kept me alive. I have night terrors almost every time I sleep even now.

"Truth be told, I kinda lost my mind for a while and when we were released I just wandered off into the countryside. I couldn't remember how to get home or even where home was. I existed on whatever I could find or steal to eat. Then one day I fell into an icy mountain stream and by the time I managed to get out my mind had cleared enough to remember Pendleton so I started home. My mental fog lifted as I traveled. I'm pretty normal, now. I've made up a few stories to tell to satisfy everyone's curiosity. Let's put the past behind us and not talk of the war ever again, not ever again." Tears glistened in Neal's eyes and his chin trembled from the strain of telling his story.

Mandy wrapped her arms around him and gently held him as he began to sob uncontrollably. Silently she prayed for a complete release of all his tormenting memories. In a few minutes she felt him relax as he choked back the last of his tears.

"I'm sorry. I didn't mean to cry, but I feel the better for

it," he said, using a ragged sleeve to wipe his face. "I guess no matter how old we get we still need a comforting shoulder from time to time."

"Tears are the heart's cleansing agent, Neal. Never be afraid to express yourself whether in joy or sorrow. I thank God He spared you. We have been praying for you and wondering what had become of you. Oh, I hear the boys. While you wash up, I will fix you some dinner. Take your time and have a good soak. I'll see you in a little while."

Mandy waited until Sam and John appeared each carrying a bucket of steaming water. Behind them Lizzie and Susan struggled with armloads of towels and soap. Katie brought up the rear, dragging a large washtub.

"You children have thought of everything. Girls, you leave the supplies on this box and come away. Neal deserves some privacy while he bathes. Sam, don't ask Neal any more questions about the war. That time is over. This is the day for making plans about the future. Do you understand?" Mandy gave the children a no-nonsense look.

"Yes, ma'am. I really don't like to hear about blood and guts, anyway." Sam blushed at his confession. "I just want the old Neal back so we can be friends again."

"That is all any of us want, Sam. You have verbalized the desires of all our hearts." Mandy took the clothes Beth had collected and laid them beside the towels.

"Scrub off the soldier person and come back to us as our beloved Neal, the farmer. We'll be waiting for you in the carriage house."

Within the hour Neal appeared at the door dressed in Smith's hand-me-downs that hung on his gaunt body like rags on a scarecrow frame. After a substantial meal during which everyone told him of the goings on in Pendleton, he went to the main house to see if his old job of plantation overseer was still available. Much to his relief Smith rehired him on the spot, scheduling a hunting trip for the following morning. Mandy breathed a sigh of relief. The sooner things returned to normal the better for everyone.

The following week passed quickly. Before Mandy knew it Christmas week was upon them. Gone were the lavish dinner parties and dances, the tables groaning with imported delicacies, the stylish ball gowns and sweet sounding orchestras. This year as in the past several years the focus was on community worship services and small family gatherings. Those who had food gladly shared with neighbors who were destitute.

To Mandy, the austere celebration of Christ's birth seemed more in character with His simple lifestyle. She enjoyed the carol singing and visitors, making the most of the season by having deeper inspirational devotions with the children.

"Miss Mandy, I saw an angel last night," announced Susan one morning as Mandy buttoned her dress.

"Really? What did he look like?"

"He had on a white robe and a gold belt. He stood at the foot of my bed and smiled at me. I think he was happy 'cause I asked Jesus to come into my heart."

"You did? How wonderful!" Mandy gathered the little girl into an enthusiastic hug. "Now you are part of God's special family with all its wonderful privileges. He will care for you like a loving father and watch over you every minute. I'm so happy! I have prayed for each one of you to come to Jesus." Mandy picked up her ward and waltzed across the room, dipping and whirling until the child giggled with delight.

With Neal home safely and Susan's commitment to Jesus,

Mandy's joy bubbled over. She sang joyful hymns and radiated a deep happiness as she sewed new doll clothes for the girls, working late at night after her regular chores were completed.

Christmas morning dawned bright and clear, the frosted fields shimmering in the sunlight as brightly as the natal star had glittered over the ancient stable. Mandy arranged her gifts at each child's breakfast plate. The girls were given rag dolls with extra dresses, hankies and carved wooden barrettes for their hair. Smith had given Mandy some tanned deer hide from which she had made the boys belts and work gloves. They politely voiced their thanks but she could see the disappointment in their eyes. After church Mandy and her children prepared to join the LaFarge family for Christmas dinner. To her delight Richard came cantering down the driveway just as they were about to enter the great house.

"Merry Christmas, Miss Mandy! I hope I'm not too late to partake of the festivities. Here is my peace offering. All you have to do is cook it." He unwrapped a fresh dressed deer from a sack behind his saddle.

"Thank you, Richard. Meat is always welcome, especially venison. Deer seem to be in short supply this year. We were just about to go in to dinner. Please come join us. Neal will hang the deer in the smokehouse, for now."

"Good to see you all in one piece, Neal. Give me ten minutes to clean up. Smith promised me his hospitality whenever I was in the area. Now I'll test his word." He handed the reins of his horse to John.

"Please stable him and give him some hay. He's had a tiring day. We rode all the way from Greenville at a steady trot." Richard patted his trusty steed on the shoulder and hurried up the steps of Smith's house.

Within minutes, he was dressed in a clean linen shirt and cord pants and surrounded by eager faces waiting to hear of his latest adventures.

"I'm surveying for the Continental Railroad while acting as an undercover agent for the army. We are trying to stop the renegade soldiers from looting and burning. Only last week we arrested a band of six. They are now languishing in the Greenville jail. I feel sorry for them in a way, they were only trying to save their farms and families by getting the means to pay their taxes and buy food, but the law must be upheld."

"Dr. Adger was visited by a group several weeks ago. They took whatever valuable items they could carry. All but one got away and he is buried in their cemetery. A tragic ending," said Mandy, reluctant to share the morbid details.

"Yes. The war has changed men's opinions of the value of life. Some find life even more sacred, while others have become hardened and kill without hesitation. May God have mercy on them and show them the error of their ways," replied Richard.

"As you have no doubt heard, Anderson is overrun with Government soldiers attempting to find Manson Jolly. His murderous escapades have increased. There is now a five thousand dollar reward on his head," he continued, soberly.

"Five thousand dollars!" exclaimed Sam. "If we could find him, we'd be rich!"

"Don't get any ideas, Sam, Manson is a very dangerous man," warned Richard. "That money would be worthless if it cost you your life. Leave him to the army. They are trained in matters like these.

"Well, enough of my stories; what is happening here?" Richard surveyed the group with interest.

"I asked Jesus into my heart and He sent me an angel,"

babbled Susan, anxious to share something of importance. "The angel was dressed in white with a gold belt and was standing by my bed."

"Well, I guess that proves we all have guardian angels," Richard said, plunking her on his lap. "That is the best news I have heard in a long while."

"My Christmas present was Neal's safe return. He will be here momentarily. Please don't say anything about the war. He doesn't want to talk about it," warned Mandy. "This is Christmas. We should be thinking happy thoughts and having you here makes me very happy." She blushed at her boldness.

As soon as Neal came to the table, the feasting began. Wild turkey, sweet potatoes, corn bread, black-eyed peas, applesauce and black walnut cake were the main fare. What did it matter if honey had been used instead of sugar or the cake had no icing. Just having everyone healthy and in good spirits was enough. When dinner ended Richard and Smith retired to the library. Neal and the boys went to start smoking the deer meat and the girls played with baby DuBois and their rag dolls.

"You seem a bit restless these days, Mandy," observed Lynette, as she and Mandy finished their tea. "Are you not happy here? Is school too much of a strain?"

"Happier now that Neal has returned. Not being able to return to Charleston has been a disappointment. Also, I feel my long stay in your carriage house is an imposition. I've tried but I have not been able to save any money from the scant wages I make teaching. There is a part of me that fiercely demands independence. I find it difficult to depend on the charity of others." Mandy gave Lynette a lop-sided smile.

"I see. Pride can be a stumbling block. What you call charity we consider good will. How sad not to be able to enjoy the benefits God provides. Without your dedication to teaching, our children would suffer greatly. We are of the mind that in providing for you, we are, in fact, providing a service to the whole community. Can you understand that?"

"Yes, I think so. It's somewhat like my taking in the homeless children at St. Phillips. In so doing I ministered to the church as a whole. I don't mean to complain, Lynette. It is so wonderful to see the children relaxed. The stress level in Charleston was fearsome. I guess I'm just ready for a change of some sort."

"Excuse me for interrupting, ladies, but the day has become so pleasant I wondered if Miss Mandy would care to take a short walk." Richard stood in the dining room doorway, smiling at Mandy.

"You go on, Mandy. I'll watch the children," urged Lynette, making a shooing motion with her hand. "Take my cloak. It's hanging by the front door."

Silently the pair walked down the porch steps to the side garden and ambled towards the woods trail. Seeing them, a blue jay cried a shrill warning to the forest creatures then flew onto a high branch to keep them under surveillance.

"I'll never forget the first time I saw you," remarked Richard, grasping her hand. "You were hovering over me spooning water into my mouth. I thought you were an angel. If it had not been for your good care, I would have died. I owe you my life, Miss Mandy. But it is not because of obligation that I speak, rather it is because I believe in you I have found a special companion. I have spent the last few months pondering and praying about my future and I must confess I do not want to continue life without you at my side." Richard stopped and leaned Mandy against a large beech tree. He placed his hands on her shoulders and searched her eyes.

"Mandy, would you do me the honor of becoming my wife? I cannot provide you with riches or a fine house but I promise to love you fervently until the day I die. I will treat your children as if they were my own: loving them, disciplining them and providing for them as well as I possibly can. For the time being we would have to stay in Pendleton as my surveying work will keep me in the area for a while. After that, we will rely on our Heavenly Father to open other doors. I'm sure this proposal comes as a surprise so take your time answering. I will be here for several days and then will return the end of January for another visit."

Mandy, speechless, stood frozen to the spot. Did she, in her heart of hearts, love this man or was she attracted to him because of the lack of other suitors? "I cannot give you an answer just now, Richard. I confess to having deep feelings for you but I must examine them and seek God's will before I give my reply. I know you believe as I do that the marriage covenant is holy and must not be broken until death claims us. Therefore we must be sure our love toward each other is strong enough to endure both the joys and sorrows of life. I confess to having a rebellious spirit when confronted with the male ego. Living with me will not be a picnic and I do not want to become a burden to you." The words seem to flow of their own accord from her constricted throat.

"It's your strong spirit I admire, Mandy. Life with me is not for the weak-willed woman as I do not plan to ever settle in a fashionable city. I love frontiers. Being an explorer appeals to me. You will probably be on your own for days at a time. That is why I think staying in Pendleton for the time being is a wise decision. Do what God tells you but know that whatever you decide, I will love you forever."

Those are the words I have longed to hear, thought Mandy as she clasped her hands around his neck and surrendered to his embrace. After a few blissful minutes, she drew back and looked at him soberly.

"Please don't volunteer as a scout to hunt for Manse Jolly," she pleaded. "I've heard Manse has killed several scouts already, besides a tax collector and several Northern soldiers. He is very dangerous, Richard. You will get no support from the local folks who consider him a hero because he is doing what they would like to do if they were not so well bred and law-abiding.

" The five thousand dollars means nothing to me. I would rather have you all in one piece and working at a less volatile occupation. You have spent years dodging bullets, now is a time for peace. Please, Richard, if you love me, leave Mr. Jolly to the authorities. The war is over. Let sleeping dogs lie."

"Manse is hardly a sleeping dog, Mandy. He is a criminal, a murderer who has taken vengeance into his own hands. He must be stopped. I have spent most of the last three years scouting in this area and know almost every cave and cove. I could be of valuable assistance." Richard's jaw tightened in rebuttal.

"I'm sure you could, Richard, but I fear for your life. If God has destined us to be husband and wife, why tempt Him by deliberately doing something that may destroy you?" Mandy searched desperately for words to validate her argument.

"On the other hand, God may use me as an instrument of His vengeance. Surely He wants this man brought to justice. Remember Psalm Ninety-one, Mandy. 'Because thou hast made the Lord, which is my refuge, even the most High, thy

Mandy's Carriage House Saga

habitation; There shall no evil befall thee, neither shall any plague come near thy tent. For He shall give his angels charge over thee, to keep thee in all thy ways.' These verses have been my watchword over the past several years. Why should I doubt them now?" Richard smiled at her gently, his blue eyes aflame with love and faith.

Tears began to trickle down Mandy's face. How could he do this? How could he wantonly jeopardize his life? Would he always be seeking a new challenge, a new frontier, regardless of his responsibilities to her and her children? Would her life as Mrs. Roberts be one of fearful waiting and loneliness as he wandered the countryside in search of one elusive adventure after another to satisfy his soul? By his own admission he expected to spend his life as an explorer. What had she gotten herself into? Perhaps Smith was right after all. She took a deep breath, brushed the tears from her face and came at the discussion from another angle.

"Promise me this, Richard: if after one attempt to capture Manse you fail to find him, you will resign as a scout for the government. You already have work suited to your abilities and personality. Surveying will keep you out in the elements you love so well and at the same time you will be contributing to the building of this nation. Isn't that what you desire? Won't that satisfy you?"

The silence seemed to stretch on forever as Richard examined her argument from every aspect. Was his desire to find Manson Jolly an ego trip or was it from God? Was he using his scouting ability as a means of living a life of solitary independence-an escape from the responsibilities having a family would require? He didn't want to hurt Mandy, he loved her, yet perhaps he was not ready for the deep commitment marriage demanded, especially when it came with a woman who easily spoke her own mind and had eight extra mouths to feed. Perhaps he had acted too hastily in asking Mandy to be his wife. He shuffled his feet restlessly as he experienced a new feeling of accountability.

"I don't know how to answer you except to say I will pray about the path my life seems to be taking. You must realize I feel a certain allegiance to the United States government since it has been my employer for some time now. It is not my style to quit when facing adversity." He took several steps backward, opening the space between them.

"I understand. Your mental strength and determination are qualities that endear you to me," Mandy said. "If you promise to pray about this situation and do whatever Gods reveals, I will accept the outcome. What choice do I have? But you must know that I will be praying, too." Mandy forced a smile to cover her disappointment.

"Well, let us leave all our decisions to the Lord for the time being. I would not want you to marry me under adverse conditions and regret your vows. By the same token, I don't want to live with a nagging wife who is determined to change me into her image of a proper husband. Perhaps we need a little more time to sort things out."

Richard spoke softly, a look of regret and resignation shadowing his face. He turned around and together they silently walked back to the carriage house where he bade everyone a hasty good-bye saying he would return in a few weeks.

Mandy's bed that night truly seemed to be made of thorns as she prayed for hours beseeching God to keep Richard in Pendleton and away from Manson Jolly. After a while, sensing in her spirit that the door of heaven was closed to her pleadings, she gave up. "Thy will be done," she whispered to the darkness.

Mandy's Carriage House Saga

On Saturday the third of January, a stranger in a black phaeton pulled by a dappled gray trotter appeared at the front gate of Meadow Wood. As Mandy watched, he slowly climbed down from the vehicle and began placing small wooden boxes at the base of the front porch steps. When he had a pile about three feet high and wide, he briskly ascended to the porch and knocked on the door.

The next few minutes passed in joyous greeting as Smith welcomed the stranger with a hearty hand shake and pat on the back, then helped the gentleman carry the boxes into the house. Together they returned to the buggy where Smith unhitched the horse and led it to the barn.

This must be a person of great importance, Mandy thought as she quickly changed from her faded day dress into her favorite blue wool with white lace collar and cuffs. Twisting her hair into a chignon, she decided she would greet the newcomer as a proper lady instead of a frumpy homemaker.

Her intuition proved correct as several hours later Smith sent one of his children to invite Mandy to tea.

"Papa said for you to come alone. The tea is for grownups only," the child said wistfully. "I think you are going to have real cake and spice tea. It's papa's cousin, Mr. Clay Malliard, who has come from Charleston. He brought us lots of goodies. Momma clapped her hands and laughed when she opened some of the boxes."

As Mandy followed the youngster into the house she was met at the door by Lynette, who whispered, "Mr. Malliard, Smith's second cousin, is here at Smith's request. His family consists of landed gentry from Tuscany, originally, and have Old World wealth. Smith hopes to interest him in purchasing the Gate's farm down the road. We would like to annex it to our property eventually. In the meantime Smith would farm it.

"Mr. Malliard is a widower. His wife died in childbirth. He would make a good husband, Mandy. He is a kind man." As Lynette spoke she urged Mandy into the parlor where a veritable feast of rich delicacies filled a silver tray.

Smith made the introductions as both men rose to their feet.

"Clay, I would like you to meet our dear family friend, Miss Mandy Greene, from Charleston, who is staying with us for a while. Miss Mandy, Mr. Clay Malliard, a cousin of mine."

Mandy offered her hand, which she had hastily scented with rose water a few minutes before.

"Dear lady, I'm happy to make your acquaintance at last," Mr. Malliard murmured, pressing her fingers to his lips. "Smith told me of your great courage and many graces but he did not mention your comely appearance."

"You are too kind, sir," Mandy replied, blushing at the rare compliment, as she sat in the chair indicated by Smith.

"Miss Mandy, Clay has generously brought us gifts of food and a host of practical items including needles, thread, glassware and even some farm supplies. Please help yourself to any of the special teas and sweets you desire. I have already filled a box for you to take home that includes sewing necessities, tea and candy for the youngsters." Smith smiled his thanks to the gentleman seated at Mandy's right, as he passed the food laden tray to Mandy and held it while she made her selection.

"Charleston is finally receiving goods from abroad again," stated Mr. Malliard. "No doubt once the low country people restock their cupboards these items and more will find their way here. We've gone long enough without the palate-pleasing foods to which we were accustomed. It's high time we returned to the menus of bygone days."

As Mandy sipped her tea, she studied her prospective beau. He was tall, dark of hair and eye and fine featured. She guessed him to be in his mid-thirties. It was obvious from the cut of the clothes that covered his muscular body that he was used to the best of everything, but there was no conceit in either his voice or his mannerisms.

"Tell me, Miss Greene, do you miss Charleston or has the upcountry air and rolling hills won your heart?" Mr. Malliard asked with a boyish smile.

"I do love Pendleton, I have found only good here, but I miss the beautiful low country houses, the smell of the salt marshes and the sprawling live oak trees. The city was so alive with culture and social events. It was a feast for the soul," she replied.

"Was is the operational word. At present there is more confusion than culture. Sad to say, some of Charleston's finest citizens now find themselves in dire straits. Many have lost their fine homes and plantations and cannot find the means to buy them back. Those who lived lavishly and had large outstanding loans on their properties have suffered the most. It seems the area is full of opportunists and unscrupulous characters just waiting to take the reins of government and possess the finest Charleston has to offer. The Queen city has been dethroned, I fear." As if saddened by the words he uttered, Mr. Malliard fell into a contemplative silence.

"I cannot believe the valiant spirit of Charleston has died. Consider what it has already been through: wars, fires, earthquakes, and yet it has always remained undaunted. I believe that wonderful city will rise again and once more be filled with beauty and delight. Charlestonians are undefeatable.

Their strong sense of family and culture cannot be obliterated no matter how contemptuous its new government. In the end, virtue will triumph; all will be well," Mandy said in a voice clear and firm. For a moment she felt as if the unseen spirit of her cousin Caroline was there, applauding her speech.

"You are a born optimist, Miss Greene. It becomes you. No wonder you are able to oversee eight children and teach school at the same time. The word 'defeat' is not in your vocabulary." The gentleman gazed at her admiringly.

"Thank you, sir." Mandy hid her embarrassment at his praise by pouring herself another cup of tea and eating a bonbon. A warm sensation spread through her. How nice it was to converse with someone who shared the same culture, who understood her heritage. She hoped Mr. Malliard would stay for a long visit.

As if reading her mind, Smith said, " Clay will be with us for a week, Mandy. If you are agreeable, come for dinner tomorrow evening. With school resuming, I realize it will be difficult to find much time for socializing, but I hope you will make yourself available to us whenever possible." He smiled pointedly at Mandy, before turning to engage his cousin in a discussion about the types of cotton and corn best suited to the area.

Mandy talked with Lynette about the school curriculum, finished her tea and returned home, carrying the wooden container overflowing with long denied delicacies.

"Look, Miss Mandy! Marmalade! Licorice drops, shortbread cookies, butterscotch taffy, pearl buttons." Katie and Beth, exclaiming in delight at the treasures within the wooden box, emptied it by laying the items one by one on the kitchen table. Their excitement soon brought Susan and Lizzie to see what was going on.

"Candy! I want candy, please." Susan stretched as tall as

she could in order to see the selection of goodies just beyond her reach.

Lizzie, her jaws working furiously as she chewed a piece of taffy, gave Susan a licorice drop.

"I don't like this," Susan said, spitting the black globe into her hand after tasting it. "I want what you have, Lizzie."

Mandy unwrapped a taffy and took the licorice from Susan's hand. After rinsing it in water, she popped it into her mouth. It would not do to waste such a delectable treat.

The following evening, after feeding her family and putting Susan and Lizzie to bed, Mandy dressed in her best winter outfit: a burgundy brocade jacket with silver buttons and a white lace jabot over a matching burgundy and black striped skirt. She worked her long, brown hair into a braided coronet on top of her head, allowing some curling tendrils to cascade around her ears. Tonight she would play the part of an available Charleston lady of breeding.

Dinner was a delightful combination of local vegetables and some of the special culinary delights Mr. Malliard had brought. Mandy ate slowly, enjoying tastes she had not experienced in years. The conversation centered on the positive aspects of the rebuilding of the South although there was not much to be said in favor of the reconstruction program as much of the tax money found its way into the pockets of the greedy politicians instead of going toward the renovating of civic buildings.

"How fares the Citadel?" Mandy asked. "Have classes begun again?" She had often wondered the fate of David Lee.

"Yes, classes began in November. At the moment the number of cadets is small. Those enrolled are helping to rebuild some of the buildings damaged by cannon fire," Mr. Malliard replied. "Most of the teachers were used as strategists during the war, but they have returned to their teaching responsibilities, now. I assume your tutoring skills will again be in demand by next year, although you may find more children from the scalawag families needing your help than those from the gentry." He shrugged as he continued, "Common people may be able to put on a pleasing veneer, but breeding will tell, every time."

"Do you know Dr. Arthur Gibbes of Beaufort?" Mandy questioned, hoping for more information about her friends. "I received a letter from them several years ago saying they had gone to Madison, Georgia to stay with a relative after their rice plantation had been destroyed."

"That was a good decision. I heard Sherman spared that town on his march to the sea because of the Northerners living there." Mr. Malliard chewed the last bite of his coconut cake thoughtfully, before continuing.

"Although Jeff Davis and his followers have sought temporary refuge in Mexico, some leaders of the old Charleston order are meeting secretly to try to restore our society to what it was before the war. Of course, according to the federal government we are not allowed to own slaves, but many of our former slaves are willing to work for a mere pittance if we will give them free shelter, since they have no schooling or special skills other than manual labor. I suspect in a few years the Old South will again be in full bloom."

Mandy cringed inwardly. How callous this man was toward the war and its many casualties. He had experienced only a minimum of discomfort and inconvenience therefore he was indifferent to the great loss suffered by many of the middle and lower classes. In Pickens District she had heard there were still several thousand residents that were penniless.[1]

---
[1] Edgar, South Carolina, A History; University of SC press, 1998 P.368

"Could the leaders of the South not plan for a new day of equal rights where each man and woman regardless of color or creed could have the right to pursue an honest livelihood without being suppressed?" she asked.

Three pairs of eyes fashioned on her in bewilderment as a weighty silence filled the room.

"Surely you jest, Miss Greene," said Mr. Malliard defensively, as he raised his hands in protest. "Our whole economy is built on cheap labor. Without it the noble class would cease to function. Our standard of life would suffer immensely as would society in general. Who supports the refuge houses and keeps the hospitals and private schools running? The wealthy, that's who! What would happen if the upper class was not able to be as philanthropic as in the past? Robberies, slums and other undesirable elements would overrun our cities. Illiteracy would abound as there would be fewer schools and probably no libraries. It would be chaos, sheer chaos!"

"But if the wealth were distributed more evenly there would be more people able to contribute to the needs of the cities," persisted Mandy. "The burden would not be just on a few. A more capable middle class would develop. In the end, even more might be done in the name of charity than has been done in the past."

"You must understand, Clay, that Mandy's early years were spent on a sharecropper's farm in Tennessee," interjected Smith quickly, before his guest could formulate a scathing reply. "She has not had the background to understand the South's very special social relationships, having lived only seven years in Charleston.

"Now, if you ladies will graciously excuse us, we will have cigars and brandy in my library. I have several propositions to go over with Clay." Smith rose hastily, scraping his chair legs along the floor in his desire to avoid any further verbal confrontation between Mandy and Mr. Malliard. His cousin followed suit, his mouth set in a thin line, indicating his displeasure.

Mandy kept her eyes downcast so they would not reveal the wrath roiling inside her. Sharecropper, indeed! It was the uncompromising, immovable, regressive convictions of men like Mr. Malliard that would keep the South in limbo for years to come, she thought, angrily.

"Miss Mandy, you must learn to curb your tongue," Lynette said in reproach. "I fear you have insulted our guest. Women of breeding do not defy tradition by discussing radical political ideas. Surely you were taught that in finishing school."

"I was taught a good many things, Lynette, but that does not mean I agreed with them all. I believe women have just as many brains and wise thoughts as men. The problem is men have been taught to regard us as the weaker sex. They assume that our mental prowess, along with everything else about us, is weaker than theirs and thus consider our opinions insignificant. The whole world suffers because women are trivialized and suppressed. It is my nature to speak my thoughts boldly and succinctly, regardless of tradition. After all, I'm just a sharecropper's daughter!" She ended her speech by bringing her fist down on the table with a bang.

"My dear, control yourself. Perhaps you are over tired," said Lynette, ringing the bell for Hannah to come clean up. "Let us both retire and get a good night's sleep. Things will look better in the morning."

Well, so much for Smith's plan to marry me off to his cousin, thought Mandy as she tossed and turned in bed. Finally, after hours of sleeplessness, she got up and knelt in prayer.

"Lord Jesus, forgive my unruly tongue. I am a stubborn, rebellious person who is as uncompromising in my opinions as are all the Clay Malliards of this world. Please turn my negative traits to positive attributes that will honor You. Grow in me the fruits of the Spirit: love, joy, peace, patience, kindness, goodness, faithfulness, gentleness and self-control; especially self-control, dear Lord.

"I know Smith meant well, but I will never be the kind of Southern lady he wishes me to be. Lord, You created me. Help me to fulfill Your plan for my life. That is all that matters. I fall so short of being a good example of Christianity. I promise I'll try harder, Jesus. In the meantime, thank You for loving me anyway.

"Please don't let Mr. Malliard be upset or think unkindly of me. I was wrong to argue. Forgive me. I am a guest here, help me to remember to act accordingly."

A few tears of frustration dropped onto the bedspread as she climbed under the covers. She sighed in despair. Would she ever be respected for her own natural God-given qualities? She closed her eyes when suddenly out of the blue it hit her: she was treating Richard in the same way Mr. Malliard was treating her. Either she accept Richard just as he was and rejoice in his uniqueness or she should value him as a friend only and get on with her life. No one has the right to suppress another, she thought, and my demands on Richard are suppressing him.

Where was her faith? Why couldn't she trust in God's goodness as she taught her children to? Hadn't she told them repeatedly either God was Lord of all or He was not Lord at all? Was hers a faith like the seed that fell in shallow soil, springing up quickly but wilting in the heat of adversity? How strange that after all she had been though, she should now doubt God's keeping power. Then the revelation came to her: she had unconsciously divided her faith between God and Richard. Part of her faith was resting on Richard's ability as a woodsman to avoid danger instead of trusting God to have His way. If Richard was killed, he would go to be with the Lord; she would be the one left to cope with living. Even so, God's blessings would not cease, nor His provisions end. Another door of opportunity would open, perhaps one even more suited to her than marriage.

Her problem was dwelling on the negative possibilities that had surfaced from fear and not so much fear for Richard as fear for herself if he did not come back to her. The whole situation revolved around self: her hopes and dreams. For a moment her soul lay naked before her eyes. It was not a pretty sight. No wonder a person, no matter how perfectly behaved, could not please God. It was the dark, hidden recesses of the soul He saw; the muddy water of self, spewing forth excuses and reasoning based on the instinct to survive. Even the words 'Thy will be done' that she had uttered just moments before contained the unspoken ending 'as long as it benefits me.'

"Give me one more chance to get it right, Lord. I'll try to do better," Mandy whispered. God's reassurance came in the form of the peace needed for sleep.

Chapter Eleven

Three weeks later, as Mandy was hanging out her washing, a strange man dressed in a dark wool jacket and cord pants with a heavy bandage on his right leg came riding up the lane on a bony, chestnut gelding. As he approached nearer, he gave a smart salute in her direction.

"Richard!" Dropping a sheet slipshod over the rope line, she rushed out to meet him just as he dismounted painfully.

"Richard! You've been injured! Oh, I'm so glad you came back. Here, sit on this bench. I'll get you a cup of coffee." Mandy's heart began to flutter at the sight of him.

"Never mind, Mandy. I'm fine. Just sit here beside me and let me look at you. There for a while I was afraid I would never see you again," he said as he pulled her down beside him.

"What happened to your leg? Where did you go?" Mandy adjusted her shawl around her shoulders and clasp his hands in hers.

"I was given a local Indian scout and two other soldiers

as a team to hunt for Mr. Jolly. That Indian had sharp eyes and followed signs I couldn't even see. We headed into the foothills. The next day as I was leading the team to a cave I knew, shots rang out so fast and accurately that we were all felled before we could shoot back. All were killed except me. The first bullet whizzed over my head because at that very moment I had bent down to adjust my saddle girth. The second shot grazed my leg and hit my horse directly in the heart, dropping him immediately. I lay half covered by my fallen horse, pretending to be dead. When night came, I wrapped my leg and made my way to a farm near the Tugaloo River. The good folks there asked no questions and helped me doctor my wound for several days because it had become infected. I bought this horse from them and returned to Anderson via the main road.

"Three men killed! What a tragedy! As of yesterday I am now a civilian. I resigned my commission. It is not my purpose to lead men into a death trap. I hate killing; that is why I became a scout. And now I am responsible for the deaths of three good men." Richard shook his head in despair and sorrow.

"You are not to blame. You were only doing your duty. The scouting party would have gone out with or without you." Mandy squeezed his hands sympathetically.

"Yes, but without me they may not have been killed. I think I unknowingly led them right into Manson's hideout." His face contorted in grief. "I'm not sure I will ever be able to forgive myself for the deaths I caused. I feel as much a murderer as the man we were hunting."

Mandy reached up to brush an unruly lock of Richard's fair hair away from his eyes. "I need to ask your forgiveness for my unkind words when we were last together, Richard. It was fear that made me speak in the way I did. I'm very sorry I upset you." Mandy laid her head against his shoulder in an act of supplication.

A gentle, healing stillness enveloped them until, from somewhere high in the sky, the shrill cry of a hawk hunting his dinner rang out. Death is all around us, thought Mandy. The whole chain of life depends on the sacrifice of one being for the benefit of another. From the tiniest insect to the very Son of God, lives are given to sustain life. Would her death someday benefit others?

"Come inside. It's getting cold out here. Thank God for your safe return. Truly He has a special plan for your life and I want to share it. Let my love be part of your healing process. I do so want to help." Rising, she pulled her beloved to his feet and supported him as he climbed the carriage house steps.

Pausing at the door, Richard turned his full gaze on Mandy and said, " I would like to ask again for your hand in marriage, Mandy. Will you favor me with an answer soon?"

"If it is alright with my children, I will be happy to be Mrs. Richard Roberts. Let's see if God will confirm our marriage through them in the next few days." Mandy gave him a quick hug and opened the door.

As they entered the parlor, Lizzie and Susan ran to meet them. They gave Richard a heartfelt welcome, sympathy for his injury and sweetness for his soul.

"Lt. Roberts has resigned his commission," Mandy announced at supper that evening. "From now on you may call him Mr. Richard, just as you call me Miss Mandy. He will be staying in Anderson for a few days until he can collect his salary from the army. Perhaps he will come for a visit once or twice while he is nearby, if you ask him nicely." Mandy gazed across the table at Richard, a twinkle in her eye.

"Indeed I shall. As a matter of fact I was hoping to take you boys hunting this week, if Mr. Lafarge will let you borrow his mule. I assume two of you could ride together? Walking is still a little difficult for me, as you can see."

"Sure we can," said John, in anticipation of the exciting event. "Sam and I ride him to the fields whenever we have to work the corn."

"Good. Alex can ride behind me. Let's go on Thursday. That will give me three days to rest up and complete my business. Be ready by nine in the morning. Agreed?"

"Yes, sir," the boys chorused in unison. It looked as if Mr. Richard was going to be as much fun as Lt. Roberts had been.

Thursday morning Sam appeared at the table dressed in heavy woolen pants and sweater. "I hope I get a turkey. They're hard to see when they are roosting in the pine trees," he announced, spooning honey over his grits. "Neal says we can't talk while we're stalking deer because they will hear us. I don't know if I can be quiet all day."

"Just keep talking now, Sam and you'll soon use up your quota of words for the day," teased Katie, ruffling his hair as she placed several slices of toast on his plate.

Alex stumbled sleepily to the table, his face aglow at the prospect of going hunting with the bigger boys. Mandy swallowed her concern that he might not be able to keep up and smiled brightly at him.

"Alex, be sure to wear a heavy sweater and cap. It's cold outside right now. Hopefully the sun will warm things up by afternoon. I've fixed you all lunches. Please ask Mr. Richard to have you back by dark." She placed a small bundle in front of each boy and gave John a canteen of water to carry.

"I wish Mr. Richard lived around here so we could see him everyday," said John. "He's nice and teaches us man things. I like that."

"I wish Mr. Richard was my father. It's been so long since I've had a father I can't hardly remember him." Sam paused, lost in thought. "Miss Mandy, do you think Mr. Richard would like to be our pretend father?"

Mandy jumped, spilling her tea. Was this God's answer to her prayer? The boys had never before so openly voiced their desire for male companionship. "It wouldn't hurt to ask, but why don't you think about it for a few days, just to be sure. Perhaps you are just excited about going hunting."

A knock on the door rescued her. It was Richard carrying several rifles and a small knapsack. "Is my crew ready? We've some serious riding to do if we are to fill the family larder. Let's go, boys. Be sure to put some waxed paper or canvas in your shoes to keep out the wet. Good morning, Miss Mandy."

"Good morning, Richard. Everyone is anxious to be off. Supper will be waiting when you get back." She watched in amusement as her clan scampered down the steps and fell in line behind their leader. Shutting the door, she turned toward the kitchen and bumped into Katie. "Excuse me. I didn't see you standing there, Katie. Will you join me for a quiet cup of tea?"

"Could I speak to you alone?" asked Katie, returning to the dining table.

"Of course. Beth, why don't you help Susan and Lizzie dress?"

Beth reluctantly left the room as Katie pulled her chair close to Mandy. "I want to go to school up North. I'm tired of all the pressures here. I want to live where people are more open-minded."

"What makes you think things are different in the Northern states?" Mandy struggled to hide her surprise and distress.

"I've been reading your history books. The people seem to have a broader vision. They honor folks who have made a valid contribution to society rather than paying homage to a family name.

"Last fall I placed an ad in several newspapers offering my services as a part time maid or nanny so I could attend a woman's college. I have received two replies. One is in Philadelphia, the other in Massachusetts. Would you like to see the letters?" Katie pulled several sheets of folded paper from her dress pocket.

Mandy slowly reached for them. The crisp paper rattled in her shaking hand. How could Katie do such a thing? Studying had been so hard for her with her dyslexia. For a moment she felt betrayed, then amazement enveloped her as she began to read.

Dear Miss Kathleen Raney,

We are replying to your query in the Concord Chronicle. My husband, who teaches at Whitehall, a military school for young men, assures me he can enroll you at The Towers, the companion finishing school for young women, for the very minimal fee of twenty dollars a month. This amount you can earn by assisting us when we hold parties and dinners (which we do almost every weekend). You will be responsible for serving and cleaning up.

We have a spare bedroom and will be happy to provide you room and board, trusting that you will be able to absorb whatever other expenses you incur. If you are interested, we will send you references.

Sincerely,
Mrs. Able Martin

Mandy's Carriage House Saga

"Is a finishing school what you had in mind? Haven't I taught you enough to prepare you for college entrance exams?" asked Mandy, defensively.

"I'm sure you have. I thought by taking a final year I would be able to brush up on some subjects I am weak in and perhaps have time to work somewhere part-time to cover my college expenses. There is a small private Methodist college nearby that offers several degrees for women. I'm not sure what I would like to study yet, but I will make a decision after I have examined their curriculum." Katie's taut voice betrayed her tension.

Mandy nodded and turned to the next letter.

To Miss K. Raney:
Dear Madam,

In answer to your ad in the Philadelphia Inquirer I am offering you a position in my millinery establishment. As you want to further your education, you would work for me from 6am to noon then attend classes at Independence Hall, a pre-university school for ladies interested in education or medical degrees.

I have a small garret room above my shop where you may stay rent-free and I will provide you with a hearty breakfast. Other living expenses must be your responsibility.

If you have further questions, please reply to the above address.

Sincerely,
Miss Rachel Toombs

"Well! Opportunities seem to abound. What have you decided to do? Are these offers sufficient? Where will you get traveling money?" Mandy passed the letters back to Katie with a flourish. She was amazed at Katie's initiative.

"I've prayed about each offer and have decided to accept the one in Concord, Massachusetts. Somehow living with a family appeals to me as I think it would be safer. I'm not sure I am prepared to go it totally alone, yet. Plus, with all the parties they hold I may meet some very interesting people and perhaps earn extra money by tending children or serving at other homes. I'm healthy and hardy. I can burn the candle at both ends for a while. I have to try this, Miss Mandy. I do not want to become a wife and mother before I've had the chance to discover myself. You understand, don't you?"

"Yes, dear, I do," replied Mandy, remembering her own search for self-identity. "When do you plan to leave? Have you written to the Martins again?"

"Yes. I should be hearing from them soon. I hope to leave in April, as soon as school is out, if possible. Do you think Mr. Richard could find any more material? I would like to take at least three nice dresses and a serviceable pair of shoes. The rest can wait. I plan to work until the beginning of the next school year so I will have enough saved to cover books and other expenses."

"It seems you've thought of everything, Katie. I'm very saddened by the thought of your leaving us but I admire your courage and determination. I'm sure the Lord will provide for your needs. I will ask Lynette if she has any dresses she no longer wants. Perhaps we can redo them for you. As for shoes, Richard can take a tracing of your foot when he goes to Greenville next. He can be trusted to select a stylish but sturdy pair of shoes for you. April is just around the corner so we will have to hustle to complete your wardrobe."

"Miss Mandy, I'm hungry!" whined Susan, sidling up to Mandy, her dress half unbuttoned and her golden hair hanging in a snarled cascade down her back.

"Goodness gracious! Look at the time. I'll fix your breakfast right away. Katie, see what you can do with Susan's hair." Mandy jumped up, grateful for the interruption. So much was happening so quickly, she needed time to sort it all out. The startling news from Katie had almost driven Richard's proposal from her mind. By afternoon her head was spinning as her thoughts bounced from one event to another.

Insisting the girls nap for an hour after dinner, she went downstairs, curled up in one of the carriages and prayed. As her prayers deepened, in her mind she saw herself and Richard standing side by side. Above them floated a large white banner with the words: 'Whoso findeth a wife, findeth a good thing and obtaineth favour of the Lord.' (Prov.18:22) A great peace filled her heart as she realized God was showing her His will. He had sent her Richard who loved her children as much as he loved her. What could be better than that? She would give him her answer tonight.

Later, as she cleaned carrots and parsnips to add to the roast that had been simmering for hours, she mentally took stock of her resources. There were several pieces of Cousin Caroline's jewelry she had been hoarding as insurance against total poverty. When these were sold they would provide Katie with traveling money and a small nest egg. She would give them to Richard to sell in Greenville as soon as possible.

The timing of her marriage would depend on how soon a house could be rented. She was not going to begin married life in the carriage house unless absolutely necessary. It was unreasonable to expect to be courted in the customary way since Richard was rarely in town. Of course she would continue teaching as long as possible. She would need a diversion if she was to be without her husband for weeks at a time.

How thankful she was that the Lord had led her to Pendleton where everyone looked out for one another. Now that returning to Charleston was impossible, she was determined to appreciate Pendleton all the more.

"Miss Mandy! The boys are back! Come see what they brought." Grabbing a cloak as she spoke, Beth dashed down the steps. As the day's harvest was unloaded from the mule's back, each boy boastfully gave a detailed account of his hunting prowess. Even little Alex had been successful at bagging several rabbits.

"I'm so proud of you, boys, and you, too, Richard. Now we have enough meat to see us through until spring!" Mandy clapped her hands in delight. "While you are washing up, I'll finish supper."

It didn't take the family long to devour every morsel Mandy had cooked. After dinner, she and Richard walked down to the stable for privacy.

"I have decided to accept your marriage proposal, Richard," Mandy said while studying his face for a reaction. "I truly believe this is God's plan for our lives. Since there is so much turmoil around us right now, I won't hold you to a long engagement or a proper courtship. All I ask is for a rented house of our own, with room enough so we can have a separate area to ourselves." She reached up and tenderly stroked his cheek.

Richard took her hand, kissing it gently. "Mandy, you have made me the happiest man on earth. I promise you the biggest house I can afford and all the trimmings that go with it. When would you like to become Mrs. Richard Roberts?"

"The middle of March. I know that is not much of an engagement period but Katie has decided to go to school in Massachusetts and wants to leave in April. I want her to share in our happiness, Richard. She is as close to me as if she were my own natural daughter. Hopefully, we will be able to find a house by March, but if not, perhaps by summer we can move. Do you want to tell the children our plans or wait awhile? Katie doesn't want them to know she is leaving; not until closer to the time in case something goes amiss."

"Let's share our happiness and get them involved right away. The more, the merrier. Everyone needs something joyful to look forward to. Our marriage will be the talk of the town, one way or the other. Some won't appreciate your marrying a Yankee, you know." Richard drew Mandy into the circle of his arms.

"Times are rough right now, but I see a new era coming; a time of great growth and discovery for this nation. The railroad will be a major player in our new-found prosperity and I am in on the ground floor. God is not through with this country, Mandy, the best is yet to come."

Mandy smiled at his positive predictions and snuggled against his shoulder. She agreed with his prophecy. Jesus held the keys to their future and His desire to bless His children was greater than their capacity to receive.

"There will be a family meeting in ten minutes," announced Mandy, hanging up her shawl as she entered the kitchen. It was hard to remain calm as Richard took the seat across from her at the table. Her heart skipped a beat every time she thought of the wedding to come and finally, a home of her own.

There was the usual scraping of chairs as the children took their places at the table. Mandy looked solemnly at each face around the circle then, unable to suppress her joy, grinned from ear to ear

"God has heard and answered our prayers," she said. "Sam,

you wanted a father; I have prayed for a husband. Mr. Richard wants to be both my dear husband and your loving father, if you agree. We are to be married in March, and we want you all to be part of the wedding."

For a brief moment no one moved as they absorbed the implications of Mandy's announcement. Then, pandemonium broke loose.

"Hurray!" shouted Sam. "I get a new dad. I'm so glad it's you, Mr. Richard. We can go hunting every day. Will you teach me to track?"

"Hush up, Sam. We are all very happy for you," said Neal, shaking Richard's hand in a manly fashion. "Miss Mandy deserves the best. We love her very much."

"Thank you, Neal. I'll try to be the best husband and father I can be. I love her with all of my heart and will do right by her, I promise."

"Will you be my daddy, too?" asked Susan, jumping down from her chair and climbing into Richard's lap.

"I'll be delighted to be daddy to all you beautiful young ladies and fine lads, but you must remember I'm new at this so you will have to cut me some slack."

"Miss Mandy will help you. She's as good a mother as we could ever have." Beth patted Mandy's arm. "Will we have fancy new dresses? Are you planning a big party?"

"Slow down, Beth," laughed Mandy. "I don't think you will need new dresses as we plan to have a very simple ceremony with just close friends attending. Then we will invite the whole town to a big reception. But since most people have few fashionable items left, we will try not to make them feel uncomfortable by wearing fancy finery. Don't you think that's a good idea?"

"I guess so." Beth tried to hide her disappointment in not

getting a fancy ball gown.

"Perhaps we can add a lace collar and cuffs to your blue checked dress. Would that help?" asked Katie, trying to sooth Beth's feelings.

"That would be nice. I'm just so tired of wearing the same three dresses. They are all getting too tight and too short," complained Beth, who envisioned herself a step above the ordinary. "My new dress is the only one that fits properly."

"Try not to grow so fast, Beth. Another inch and you will be as tall as I am," said Mandy, giving her a quick hug. "Now, who wants to help me plan the wedding?"

"Let's go, boys. This is strictly women's work. We ought to check on the meat in the smokehouse, anyway." Richard hustled his group out the door before Mandy could object.

"Well! Women's work, indeed. This is not work, it's fun. Why don't we plan a pretend wedding first and include all the fancies we can think of. Then we'll get serious about the whole affair. Let's see, my gown will be imported silk with a lace train ten feet long." Mandy closed her eyes to concentrate. "Lizzie will be the train bearer while Susan walks in front of me throwing jewels and flower petals along my path."

"You ought to wear a diamond tiara and a pearl necklace," suggested Katie. " I will be clothed in a gauzy green dress with sparkles all down the front. The boys will be dressed in gray velvet jackets and pants and white silk shirts."

"I want to wear red shoes with silver buckles," added Lizzie. "And I want my dolly to have red shoes, too."

It took an hour to design the make-believe wedding and less than twenty minutes to finalize the plans for the real one. The wedding would be at the church closest to the center of town with the Reverend Adger officiating. The reception would be a potluck dinner and the happy couple would go for a two-day honeymoon at a secret location.

When the itinerary was explained to Richard and the boys, they thought it very satisfactory, secretly glad to avoid as much pomp and circumstance as possible. It was decided the children would act as bridesmaids and groomsmen. Richard suggested Smith LaFarge escort Mandy down the aisle and she heartily agreed.

Richard left the next morning to continue his surveying for the railroad, promising to return by the end of February. Mandy hated to see him go but now the days did not seem long enough for all she had to do.

On Sunday Lynette brought Mandy four yards of a fine, white, tatted lace border.

"Oh, how beautiful," exclaimed Mandy, holding the lace against the dark background of her skirt. "Where did you ever find such an intricate design?"

"I took if off an old tablecloth I had," confessed Lynette. "The linen was beginning to fray so I had stopped using it. The lace will do for collars and cuffs, don't you think?"

"Of course. There is enough here for all the girls. How lovely it will be for them to have matching accessories. Thank you so much." Mandy carefully folded the lace.

"I have one other item. You could call it the 'something blue' for your wedding." Lynette carefully unwrapped a large bundle and held up a gown of cornflower blue water-stain taffeta. "Smith bought this for me just before I became pregnant the last time. I never wore it because the color didn't suit me and now I am too thick in the waist to fit into it. I know you are several inches taller than I am but perhaps we could sew in a white lace cummerbund or something to extend the bodice."

Mandy fingered the crisp material. Blue was her favorite

Mandy's Carriage House Saga

color. She hesitated, unsure of what to do. Was the material too grandiose for a wedding dress?

"Please take it, Mandy. A bride should look her best on her wedding day. Everyone will feel so much better seeing you dressed for the occasion. I know how you feel about putting on airs, but it's the most important event of your life." Lynette thrust the dress into Mandy's arms.

"I'm overwhelmed. The color is perfect for me and I'm sure I can alter it to fit. Oh, Lynette, God bless you!" Mandy pressed her cheek against Lynette's, tears sparkling in her eyes. She felt so loved.

That weekend she planned her teaching schedule for the next two months. Once April arrived, school would close so the local children could help with the planting of fields and gardens. It was best to concentrate on her lessons now rather than after the wedding when she might be distracted by new experiences and emotions.

True to his word, Richard appeared the last week of February, a huge sack slung behind his saddle. With exaggerated huffing and puffing, much to the delight of the smaller children, he hauled it up the carriage house steps and into the parlor.

"What wonderful goodies do you suppose I have in here?" he teased, slowly untying the bindings. "Well, where did this come from?" He held up a pair of brown serge trousers, then another and another. "I do believe there is a pair for each young man and a fancy cream linen shirt to match," he said, passing the clothing to eager, outstretched hands.

"Don't worry, I haven't forgotten the ladies but I wasn't sure of sizes so I bought material. You will have to make your own dresses. I brought a magazine showing the latest styles so you will be right in fashion. Does that please you, Miss

Beth?" Richard opened a well-wrapped package to reveal yards of rose-colored linen.

"Oh, how beautiful," Beth said, "Thank you, Mr. Roberts, for thinking of us."

One piece of soft, white batiste remained. Richard, bowing gracefully, offered it to Mandy. "Pure white for the pure in heart," he said with a smile that sent her insides quivering.

"Thank you, Richard. I shall make good use of this," she replied, blushing at the thought of making it into a fancy nightgown and shift for her honeymoon.

"The best is yet to come. If you ladies and gentlemen will gather your wraps, I suggest we all go for a stroll down Cherry Street."

Mandy's heart began to pound with anticipation. Could it be Richard had found a house to rent? She clutched his arm as they hurried along. The mile walk to town seemed endless. Then suddenly he stopped in front of a single story house with a long, low front porch and a wing on either side. Red camellias bloomed by the front door and cream-colored witch hazel blossoms decorated the side yard.

"My dear family, this is your new home. That is, if Miss Mandy approves," he said, throwing open the front door. Mandy hesitantly shuffled forward as if afraid everything would magically disappear. Standing at the doorway, she carefully peered into the dimly lit hallway. Impatiently the children scurried past her, dashing about from room to room.

"It has four bedrooms and two parlors," Richard murmured in her ear. "There is no dining room but the kitchen is very spacious and an indoor bathroom has been added on. Do you like it?"

Mandy wandered slowly through the house, touching a window, stroking one of the carved walnut mantels. This was the Clark house. She had heard that, after the death of her husband, Mrs. Clark had moved to Summerville to be near her daughter.

Light streamed in the tall, narrow windows casting a golden glow on the heart pine floors. Tapestry drapes, a bit faded, graced the front windows while wooden shutters offered privacy in the bedrooms. The parlor walls were tastefully papered in light gray swirls on a medium blue background. In the kitchen she found a hand pump at the sink. The wood stove was tucked into a corner that had been lined with brick to prevent the walls from overheating.

"It's lovely," she stammered. "Can we afford the rent? It seems so grand."

"There is no rent. I bought it outright. The railroad advanced me a goodly sum and I had a substantial nest egg saved from the sale of my Pennsylvania farm. What furniture you see goes with the house. The rest we can add as time goes on."

Slowly it dawned on her. This was her house – all hers, and debt free. "Oh, Richard! Thank you, thank you! I never dreamed of living in such a fine house. Even the bedrooms are spacious. It's beyond my wildest imaginings!"

"I hope you are always this easy to please," he laughed, delighted with his success at house hunting. "Here are the keys. You may do what you wish inside as long as you don't chop down any of the shrubs or trees. I am quite fond of the landscaping."

"I promise not to touch even so much as a lowly weed. Really, it's very clean. There won't be much work involved before we can move in. I would prefer to live here for a while to get a feel for the house before I decorate."

"A wise decision. What's all the ruckus about? Where

are the boys?"

At that moment Beth appeared in the doorway. "Miss Mandy, John and Sam want the same bedroom Katie and I do. Come tell them they can't have it."

"Please don't spoil this wonderful surprise by arguing. We will discuss it later," Mandy said, decisively. "Let's look around the yard then we must go home before it gets dark. Hurry now!"

The grounds were well designed and included many blooming shrubs and several fruit trees. Mandy could see clumps of daffodils emerging from the red clay soil and what looked like the remains of a herb garden near the kitchen door. A grape arbor containing a small bench added an intimate touch.

"We'll need a rope swing on that large oak branch," Richard mused, "and a joggling board for the girls."

"Can we have some chickens?" asked Sam. "Where should I start my bug collection? Can we have our own dog?"

"Keep the bugs away from the house. I suppose we could have a few hens. Remember, we are living in town so our menagerie must be kept to a minimum." Richard frowned slightly as he mentally placed a henhouse at the far end of the side yard.

With a sheepish look on her face, Beth walked up to Mandy. "Is it all right to pick some of the flowers?" Several clusters of red camellias were clutched in her hand.

"It looks like the deed is already done," remarked Mandy. "Come, let's go home and put them in water."

Talk of the new house was on everyone's lips. Mandy noticed Katie had been unusually quiet during the whole episode. She dropped back to walk with her.

"Katie, the time has come to tell everyone of your plans,

especially now that we have to divide up bedrooms. Are you having second thoughts about leaving? You don't have to go, you know. There are schools nearby that would welcome you."

"I'm certain my decision to leave is right for me. It's just that I will miss so many new adventures with the family. I'm homesick already and I haven't even left yet."

Mandy threw an arm around Katie's shoulder. "You will soon be having wonderful adventures of your own. But remember, we will always be here for you and will welcome your return."

After the supper dishes had been cleared away, Mandy called the children to attention. "As I promised, we will discuss the living arrangements, but first, Katie has something to say."

"I'm moving to Massachusetts where I plan to go to school. I will be living with a married couple who are both teachers. I will be leaving in April," she blurted out, her cheeks aflame with embarrassment.

The children stared at her as if unable to believe their ears. Finally Susan, who depended on Katie's loving care, said, "Can I go with you?"

"No. This is something I must do myself, Susan. You'll understand when you grow up." Now that the announcement had been made, she felt a sense of relief.

"You're not mad at us, are you?" asked Sam.

"Of course not. I'm nearly a grown-up and I want to chart my own course."

"Well, that leaves one less person to take up room in a bedroom," stated John, always the practical one. "You three girls can have the biggest room and we boys can divide up: Neal and I in one room; Alex and Sam in the other."

"We'll need a bigger closet then or a chest to put our things in," replied Beth, willing to see the wisdom in John's plan.

"That you shall have," promised Richard. "I'll see to it right away. Miss Katie, we all wish you much success. You are a very bright young lady and with the Lord on your side I'm sure everything will turn out just fine."

"What a wonderful day this has been. I think we ought to take a moment to thank God for his blessings. We have lovely new clothes and a wonderful house to live in. What more could we want? Let's do a round-robin prayer," urged Mandy.

Every head bowed as each person voiced his own prayer of thanksgiving. Richard ended the session by praying for Katie's safety and also for the peace and healing of the nation. Knowing she was marrying a godly man who felt comfortable praying out loud brought great peace to Mandy's heart. More and more God was showing her this marriage was part of His plan for her life.

The week before the wedding was a madhouse. Her students shyly left simply wrapped presents of napkins, carved wooden spoons, tatted doilies, etc. on her desk. Church friends, anxious to provide whatever food they could for the reception inquired as to her needs. Several women offered their services as dressmakers so Mandy gratefully assigned them the task of making the girls new dresses. In her spare time she cleaned and prepared their new house so it would be ready to move into as soon as she and Richard returned from their honeymoon.

Finally the big day arrived. After a large breakfast to hold everyone over until the reception, Mandy laid out her wedding clothes, packed a small trunk for her honeymoon and began to arrange her hair.

"Katie, I'm putting you and Beth in charge of the younger ones. Please make sure they are dressed and ready to leave for the church by one o'clock," she instructed. "I'll double check the boys after they are dressed. Give me an hour of peace and quiet so I can gather my wits about me. I'd like to enter the church reverently composed, not in total confusion. Have you seen Richard today?"

"Yes, ma'am. He stayed at the hotel last night because it's bad luck to see the bride on her wedding day before the service," Katie replied.

"Bad luck for whom? I wonder how many men have panicked at the last minute and left town before the ceremonies," Mandy muttered, nervously twisting her hankie.

"You know Mr. Richard would never do that," said Beth. "He loves us and wants us for his family. He said I could call him 'daddy' if I wanted to and I do. It will be nice having a father. Half the girls in church don't have fathers anymore since the war. I was three when my daddy died. I don't remember him but I remember my mama crying for days. I didn't understand what had happened. My aunt scared me by saying my daddy had gone far away and wouldn't be coming back. I wish I had known about Jesus and heaven then. It would have been such a comfort. For years I was afraid mama would go away, too, and leave me all alone. When she died, God gave me you, Miss Mandy, and I've never been afraid since. You are a wonderful substitute mother; I love you very much."

"Bless you, child. I love you, too," stammered Mandy, completely taken aback by Beth's long speech. "You children are as much mine as if I had birthed each one of you. I consider you even more special because I believe God picked you out especially for me. Now, Richard will bring us additional love and joy. God is so good! Off you go; see to the girls." She gave Beth an affectionate push toward Katie.

As they left, she sat on the edge of the bed, trembling

with anticipation. "Dear Jesus, please let everything run smoothly today. Help me not to be afraid to be a loving wife and companion. I've waited so long for this day and now that it's here I want to enjoy every moment. Let our wedding ceremony reflect the love we have for each other and for all your people. Touch hearts, Lord. May this be a time of healing for our community."

Mandy was well aware of the suppressed anger many of the town folk had because she was marrying a Union soldier. Although word of Richard's exploits to save Smith's farm and his rescue of Mandy from the bootleggers had circulated freely among Pendleton's residents, she knew some families would refuse to join her celebration or have anything further to do with her because of ill feelings toward the North.

Precisely at one o'clock Smith parked his best buggy at the door of the carriage house and helped Mandy and her troupe aboard. With a crack of his whip, he set the horses trotting briskly toward town, the cool air reddening cheeks and calming nerves. After entering at the side door of the church, Mandy smoothed down the boys' cowlicks, straightened sashes and then stood quietly by the door of the sanctuary awaiting her cue to send the children in pair by pair.

"Richard's here," announced John, his face pressed to the window. "My, he looks grand. He's got new boots, black and shiny."

Mandy's heart jumped for joy. Someone came to the door and thrust several branches of red camellias tied with a white ribbon into her arms.

"We're ready," said Smith, opening the door to the strains of a majestic hymn played on the reed organ. Alex and Lizzie, Susan and Sam, John and Beth, Neal and Katie, slowly each twosome marched down the aisle, dividing at the altar to leave space for the bride and groom.

Mandy took a deep, steadying breath, placed her hand on Smith's forearm and began the walk to a new and promising future.

"Whom God hath joined together, let not man pull asunder." (Matt.19:6)

Janet Baughman welcomes your comments. You may contact her at (864) 224-0621 to order additional books, or schedule a speaking engagement, or use her e-mail address:

janjer7@juno.com

310 Quail Run
Anderson, SC 29621